PUBLISHED

Lati`a D. Johnson

www.JohnsonPublicationsBooks.com

ISBN 978-0-98-404167-1
Published by: Johnson Publications
Newtown Square PA

Cover Layout/Design by Designs by SheShe
Editors: Carla Dean

Printed in the United States of America

Dedication

This book is dedicated to my Sons Aaron and Te`ron. You both give me the motivation to continue on my pursuit of greatness, so you both may taste the sweet fruits of my labor.

Thank You

I thank God for my gift of writing among others. My gifts were provided to me in my mother's womb and because of this I have purpose. I thank my family, friends and readers for all of their support. I would also like to thank my graphic designer Shenna for always understanding my vision and executing it with precision every time. Editor Carla Dean, your work ethic is superb and your attention to detail is appreciated. Last but definitely not least My hubby Ron. Thank you for loving me beyond measure and looking at me as if I'm the best girl in the world. Your support and patience are greatly appreciated!

PUBLISHED

Lati`a D. Johnson

INTRO

Dear Diary,

Today, I start a new life. Out with the old, in with the new. My suffering is over. No more using my looks to get what I want. No more sex for money, and most of all, no more Jerome. Today, I will take control of my fate and start the writing career I've always wanted.

Truly yours,
~~Bre~~ correction Aubrey♥

✶ ✶ ✶ ✶ ✶

The red light from Jerome's bedroom lamp framed her body perfectly. Her long, black hair and diamond studded stilettos were a turn-on for most men. She wore nothing but a smile, enticing him and making him feel as if he were the only one in the world. She knew how to do that so well. Tonight was no different. In Jerome's eyes, he wanted what was his, or at least what he felt he owned.

Aubrey did something a little different. She stopped and stared out of the window, taking it all in. This would be the night she broke free of this lifestyle and started fresh. As long as Quanda stuck to the plan, everything would work out just fine. The Atlanta skyline went from being purple to pink as the day turned into night. The city skyline, which could be seen from Jerome's window, made for a beautiful backdrop.

Aubrey continued to dance seductively and play with her tongue ring in a circular motion.

Jerome smiled. "You're one of my best bitches in the Mouse Trap. That's why you got to get it at least three times a week."

Just hearing those words made Aubrey's skin crawl. She thought about how she got into the situation she was in. She went from being one of the baddest, most wanted chicks in the ATL to dancing and being forced to trick. Not to mention giving out freebies to fat-ass Jerome on a regular basis.

Jerome was the owner of a popular strip joint in Atlanta, and Aubrey was one of his moneymakers. Aubrey was no fool. She did not mind tricking, but not at a sleazy strip joint. Her idea of tricking was getting a man with money and living it up. She figured her man should pay for all of her sugar she was dishing out.

As the song continued playing in the background, Aubrey anticipated the cue for Quanda to join the party. Shortly after that, Jerome would get what was coming to him. Jerome started to grow impatient, though.

"Damn, bitch, what are you waiting for? Come over here and sit on all this." He gestured toward his naked mid-section, where his penis was hiding somewhere under his sweaty gut.

"Come on, girl. You got to be at the club in two hours, and I want to take my time with you!"

Aubrey bit her bottom lip. Screwing him one last time had not been what she planned. As she slowly approached Jerome, he grew more excited. By the time Aubrey made it to the foot of the bed, Jerome was laying in the middle of it breathing extremely heavy.

When the words to Kelly Rowland's "Motivation" started playing on the IPod, Aubrey's eyes lit up, because she knew this torture would be over soon. She climbed up on the bed and began to gyrate. Just then, there was a thump on the front door of his condo.

Aubrey looked up at Jerome and said, "Mmmm...I got a surprise for you."

Jerome rubbed his throbbing rod. "This had better be a good one," he replied. "You know I don't like surprises."

She looked back and grinned. "Oh, trust me. You're gonna love this one."

Aubrey opened the door for Quanda and walked away. As she headed back toward the bedroom, she saw Jerome standing in the hallway with his dick still brick hard. She almost felt bad that she was going to take all of his money and then leave the Mouse Trap for good.

"What, you missed me, baby?" she asked in her seductive voice.

Before she could go into full act, Quanda stepped from behind Jerome with tears in her eyes.

"Bre, I'm sorry," Quanda yelled. "He threatened to kill me and my two kids if I ever crossed him. I couldn't take that chance!"

3

Not knowing her fate, Aubrey stood with tears streaming down her face. She had not felt that much hatred for someone since her mother ran away with a new man years ago, leaving Aubrey's grandmother to finish raising her. Aubrey's first instinct was to run, but when she turned around, she could not believe her eyes. The guest she let in was not who she had invited. There stood three big men staring at her with lust-filled eyes. One of them she recognized as a weird sexual deviant from the club.

Quanda attempted to leave as if her job was done, but Jerome grabbed her by the throat and ushered into the bedroom, where he shoved her down in a wooden chair and forced her to view the show. Aubrey yelled, screamed, and pleaded to be let go. The tall, burly guy carried her to the bed, ignoring her request. Quanda sat slumped over as she continued to cry and watch them have their way with Aubrey.

Jerome went first, and then the burly guy and "Rob the pervert" pulled a train. Rob, a regular at the club, had a stare that would make any woman's skin crawl. Jerome talked to Quanda and Aubrey as his stiff wood went in and out of her.

"Next time, you'll think twice about setting someone up," he said in between grunts. "And, Quanda, this same thing will happen to you if you ever try to cross me in your life."

Jerome had the soul of a demon. He wanted to humiliate and break Aubrey's spirit to be sure she knew who was boss. He grabbed for one of his sex toys and gestured for Quanda to join them. With her body still shaking, Quanda walked slowly toward the bed. Jerome made her join in, while he and Rob held Aubrey down. At that point, Aubrey was exhausted; her body could not take another stroke. She became numb as the moans and groans turned into background noise.

After the men were done, they were dismissed by Jerome, while Quanda was kept around for some more fun. As Aubrey lay on the floor of his room passed out and naked, Jerome went to the bathroom and replenished his Viagra cocktail. He was now ready to experience some consensual sex with Quanda. Jerome emerged from the bathroom refreshed as if nothing just happened. He noticed the look of nervousness on Quanda's face.

"What are we going to do about her, Jerome?" Quanda asked in a meek voice, trying not to make him angry.

Jerome nudged Aubrey. "She'll be knocked out until the morning. Stop being so sensitive. I've seen Bre screw more guys than she just did in this one night. She'll be fine," he responded nonchalantly.

Quanda could not believe his response. As she sat there in a daze, Jerome opened up the bedroom door and gestured for Quanda to follow him. Their party was moved to the living room.

Jerome and Quanda had been through a lot together, and the rumor was that one of her children was his. Being the devil that he was, Jerome would never claim her bastard child. No, never from a stripper hoe, as if he was any better.

Jerome and Quanda began their session, and Quanda's screams of pleasure echoed off of the walls. Inside, she was empty, hating her life and more importantly, hating the fact that she had betrayed a friend. Their session went on as planned. She drifted away in physical pleasure.

Jerome's hips moved as if they had a motor in them. He had been at it for a while and was soon ready to explode. So, he flipped Quanda around and hit her moist box doggie style. His pace quickened as he got closer to home!

"Oh...oh...oh!" he yelled out. Quanda matched his screams. The last oh sounded faint and his hip motion began to slow down. Having reached her peak, Quanda fell down face first on the sofa. Jerome's body collapsed on Quanda's back so hard that he knocked the wind out of her.

"Get up!" she yelled, while rolling over.

Jerome's lifeless body dropped to the floor with a loud thump. There lay Jerome foaming at the mouth with a silver wire wrapped around his neck, and Aubrey standing over him naked and battered.

Quanda released a loud scream of fear. The rage that reflected from Aubrey's eyes sent chills up her spine. Quanda attempted to run, but although wounded, Aubrey was too quick for her.

"Get back over here, you slimy bitch! You're going to wish Jerome got to yo' ass like he promised when I'm done with you and your kids! I stood and watched as you made love to that demon after what he did to me! You will pay with your life!"

Aubrey spit in Quanda's face.

"Since I know now that you were sooooo close to his nasty ass, I can use you for what I need."

Aubrey drug a kicking and crying Quanda to the bedroom by her hair.

"Now, you got two choices: die or die! But, before you do, you're going to open the safe for me, Mrs. Jerome Kobbs."

Quanda gathered up enough breath to say, "If you're going to kill me anyway, why would I help you?"

Aubrey stared at her with a devilish grin, the gun she had retrieved from Jerome's nightstand pointed directly at Quanda.

Bang! Bang! Aubrey put two bullets in Quanda, one in each leg. Quanda yelled out in agony. She looked at Quanda's weak body and said, "Because I can either kill you slow or fast. It's up to you. Combination, please!"

"Why are you doing this to me? I tried to help you!"

Aubrey replied, "So, you think fucking me with an oversized dildo is help? I don't think so! Combo or your toes go next."

A broken down Quanda crawled to Jerome's hiding place and tapped twice; out popped a secret drawer. Aubrey was confused. She got close to Quanda's face and grabbed her by the neck.

"I thought you said he had a safe with a combination. What the hell is this little box?"

When Quanda opened the box, Aubrey let her go. Inside was the key for his home safe, a key and combination to an off-site safe, and a GPS code.

Aubrey gathered her clothes and all of her belongings. She then filled her dance bag with all of Jerome's cash. Loaded with cash and new possibilities, Aubrey walked toward the front door. Quanda had crawled away and was now on the living room floor still bleeding. She was relieved Aubrey had spared her life. Aubrey hurried as the door became closer in view. Before exiting, she turned and fired three more rounds into Quanda, giving her the same fate as her sick, twisted Jerome.

Chapter 1
New Horizons

The screeching sound from the train's brakes startled Aubrey. She awoke and glared out of the window, as if searching the dark night for a stalker. When she realized the train had come to a complete stop, she was relieved. Sweating and grabbing her chest, she attempted to gather her thoughts. The pounding of her heartbeat reminded her of why she had to leave her hometown and travel thousands of miles to start fresh.

Aubrey stretched her long legs and let out a big sigh. She began to notice everyone around her gathering their bags and carryon items. While the entire train congregation seemed to move quickly, hurrying to meet their loved ones who were awaiting their arrival, Aubrey moved in slow motion.

As she stood up to gather her bags, her pad and pen fell to the floor. She had been jotting down ideas for her next big story. This writing thing was all new to her. She hadn't used her brain for something positive in a long time. Aubrey had always loved writing, but never pursued it. She never forgot her mother's advice to use her beauty as a weapon. She would always have to act like she was not interested in school to please her less educated mother, which up until a few months ago had always worked out for her.

Aubrey came from a long line of beauties. Her grandmother, mother, and all of her aunts were known for mesmerizing men and getting what they wanted. Aubrey had the "green trait", as well, but her beauty was far more exotic. A product of a fair-skinned mother and a full-blooded, dark-skinned Indian father, Aubrey was the perfect mixture. Her skin was a tanned bronze, and she had jet-black thick curls that fell to the middle of her back. Aubrey's eyes were grey, and her frame was five-feet, nine-inches of thickness. She was gorgeous and she knew it.

Aubrey continued to gather her belongings as the number of occupants on the train car lessened. She was the last one left to exit, and as she struggled with her overstuffed Belvah bag, a loud voice startled her.

"Ma'am, we have to clear this car for cleaning!" a voice yelled from the back of the car.

She pulled strength from within and hoisted the bag, being careful not to spill its contents. Aubrey knew she would have to get off eventually and face the new life she so longed for...

The blustery air had frozen the water on the light poles into icicles. The temperature read twenty-eight degrees on Scottie's phone. As he hurried to his black and chromed-out

Jaguar, his breath was visible for all to see. The winter in Philadelphia was brutal, and it did not excuse those with money from its bitterness.

"Shit, I should have worn a bear suit instead of these damn sweats," Scottie said out loud.

He grabbed at the crotch of his pants, while looking down as if checking to make sure his love muscle had not frozen and broke off. Scott Williams or Scottie Blaze as he was affectionately known by all of his friends was in a hurry to make it out of the cold, when he realized he had left his keys on the front counter back in the gym.

"Nooooo! Not this shit again!" he yelled with disgust.

He knew he had to go back into the gym and retrieve his keys if he was to ever make it home. So, Scottie turned quickly and began to take off. As he ran toward the gym, Aubrey stood on the corner of 30th and Market searching for five-star hotels on her cell phone. Scottie ran by so fast that the gust of wind took Aubrey's breath away and almost knocked her over.

"Damn! Next time warn me if you gonna tilt a bitch ova!" Aubrey yelled.

Scottie turned around, prepared to be his arrogant self, but found himself dumbfounded. Aubrey's striking looks were something he had never seen. What was more mind blowing to him was her southern drawl. Aubrey looked foreign, but definitely not southern. Scottie went into complete mack mode, forgetting he could get frostbite just by standing outside in that weather for more than two minutes.

He bent down and attempted to help Aubrey gather her items off of the ground. "I'm sorry for the trouble, Ma, but what I'm not sorry about is meeting you."

Aubrey looked at him as if she smelled something stank. "Is that the best you can do?"

Always ready for a battle, Scottie countered with, "Give me your number, and I can show you that I can do a lot better than that!"

Aubrey chuckled. "Boy, please"

Scottie looked down at the ground to be sure she had everything. "Is that how you treat a resident of a city you are new in?"

Aubrey ignored his continued advances as she walked away.

"Let me show you my city!" Scottie yelled from behind her.

Now annoyed, Aubrey checked her bag to make sure it did not get wet and then yelled back, "Hell naw! You're not my type!" She walked away whispering, "Broke ass."

Scottie continued on his way, confused at how rude she seemed.

As he continued toward the gym, Scottie couldn't stop thinking about how beautiful Aubrey was. Damn! I didn't even get her name! he thought to himself.

Scottie retrieved his keys and made it back to his car safely. With ice nearly covering everything, including the roads, he took his time driving home in his prized possession. The weatherman was calling for a blizzard, and he was not going to get caught outside. He turned up his stereo, blasting Rick Ross so loud that the windows of the car shook, and thought about the chance he just missed with his mystery girl.

Scottie was no slouch when it came to looks. He was used to bagging any girl he had his eye on. Aubrey was different, though. He saw her as a challenge, which made things more interesting. It was more than her beauty. He saw something else in her eyes. Scottie was far from being a dumb man; he had brains and good looks. Not the sweet, girly look like Ginuwine or Prince. No, he was all man--sexy and rugged like Morris Chestnut.

Scottie made plenty of money and knew how to spend it. He graduated from Temple University at the top of his class with a Master's degree in Business. Being from the hood gave him an edge that most smart business men did not possess. He had friends from all walks of life. Guys liked him because he was cool, and women dug him because he was sexy and rich. Scottie was one of the youngest successful entrepreneurs in Philadelphia. At the young age of twenty-eight, he owned five nightclubs and had his hands in a few other business ventures. The youngest of his parent's three sons, Scottie was his mother's pride and joy.

Scottie pulled up to his five-car driveway nestled in prestigious Radnor, Pennsylvania, located minutes outside of the inner city of Philadelphia. Scottie had three houses in the suburbs and two condos in Center City, Philly for fun. As he pulled into his parking spot, his tires crackled on the newly formed slush that had formed from the snow still falling from the sky.

Seeing headlights behind him, he immediately reached for his glove compartment. Educated, Scottie had left the hood, but the hood had not left him. As the lights dimmed and the vehicle got closer, he breathed a sigh of relief. He recognized the cream Range Rover trimmed in chrome. He had forgotten about his business meeting with his former classmate, who was now his right-hand partner.

Scottie jumped out of his car as he watched the door fly open to the Range Rover. One leg at a time, Brooke exited her vehicle, being careful not to scuff her Christian Louboutin boots. Scottie looked at her and shook his head.

"Why the hell are you wearing those damn boots in this weather?"

Brooke lifted her leg straight up in the air to show them off and yelled, "Look, tread on the bottom!"

"Just keep your leg down, 'cause you ain't getting no workman's comp or liability from my ass," Scottie replied.

They both laughed while entering the lavish home. Brooke was there to discuss one of Club Intoxic's biggest events of the year. It was time to get down to business, as Scottie planned to take over Philly one nightclub at a time.

Across town...

Aubrey was freezing. She had expended all possibilities of hotels. With her taste and money, she wanted nothing less than five stars. She gripped her BlackBerry tight and hoped for a miracle. All at once, the words "Ritz Carlton" flashed across her screen. She read the description and proceeded to call for a quickie reservation. The deal was sealed, and she was on her way to stay in the penthouse suite.

Aubrey's breath could be seen with each exhale. She scanned the area wondering where all of the cabs were. After looking through her phone to try to locate the number for a local cab company, she noticed a Yellow Cab dropping a lady off at the train station.

"Helloooooo! Over here, cabby! Yooohooo, over here!" Aubrey yelled at the top of her lungs with a thick, country drawl.

The cab driver noticed her in his rearview mirror and quickly made a U-turn to pick up his next fare. Aubrey breathed a sigh of relief as the cab pulled up directly in front of her. Aubrey struggled with her bags, while the cab driver just sat there looking over his shoulder.

"Damn, can you earn your money and get out to help a bitch?"

Aubrey attempted to put a little fire under the cab driver as she pointed out that he should have gotten out to assist her with the luggage. However, he did not move an inch.

Once she got everything inside of the cab, the driver quickly said with a strong accent, "Where to?"

Aubrey rolled her eyes, let out a sigh, and simply responded, "The Ritz Carlton Center City."

The cab driver's eyes lit up. He knew only the wealthy stayed at the Ritz; he also knew he had just screwed up his tip.

Noticing his look, Aubrey chuckled to herself and then said out loud, "There goes ya tip, sucka!"

Her arms still shaking and legs stiff from the cold, Aubrey decided to sit back and enjoy the heat, while taking in the scenery.

* * * * *

Brooke sat across from Scottie as he talked about the investment party they were planning for his latest venture, Club Intoxic. He had a huge grand opening event planned and was prepared to pull out all of the stops. Brooke was very good at getting Scottie what he wanted and pulling luxurious events off seamlessly. Scottie sat in his black wing chair jotting down notes and important dates. Brooke had been talking for over ten minutes, and he hadn't even looked up at her. She called his name three times as he stared into space.

"Scottie! What the hell has you in la-la land? Or should I say, who the hell has you there?"

Scottie snapped out of his trance and looked Brooke in the face. "What are you calling my name like that for? I'm right the hell here, not outside!"

"Yeah, your body is here, but not your mind. What girl has that nose wide open now?" Brooke said, almost sounding jealous. "Look, now is not the time for one of your three-week flings We have too much riding on this new club, which needs all of your attention."

Scottie sat straight up, trying not to let on to Brooke that she was right about him pining over a female. "Last time I checked, you worked for me. I don't take orders from your ass! Get your shit in order."

Brooke stood up, placed her hands on her hips, and said, "And the last time I checked, you don't pay me to get talked to like that, nigga. So, you better get yo' shit together!"

They both looked at each other for a moment and then began to laugh.

Scottie broke his laughter with, "I should have left your ass at Temple in that broken down Chevy where I found you. I bet you wouldn't have those boots on right now, wit' ya broke ass!"

Being the smartass she was, Brooke shot back, "Your life would fall apart without me."

Brooke's statement was half true. Scottie and Brooke had a need for one another. Brooklyn Stevens was a smart, beautiful girl who had worked hard to get where she was in life. Brooke met Scottie while attending Temple University for marketing. Brooke transferred to Temple in her sophomore year and set the men on campus on fire. Brooke stood five-feet, six-inches tall and had light brown skin with long chestnut brown hair. She wore very little make-up and had a body of a Sports Illustrated model. She and Scottie had a few classes together and an unspoken sexual tension between them. Brooke was not too open with people when she first transferred and seemed to be hiding something. Scottie, however, had been able to get closer to Brooke than most guys that were crazy over her.

Brooke was a natural beauty and that turned Scottie on. She also was not afraid to be her true self around any guy. Scottie had feelings for Brooke ever since they hung out in college, but being the ladies' man, Scottie had hit on one of Brooke's friends from her dorm, and they kicked it for a few dates. From that point on, Brooke always kept Scottie in the "friend" category. Scottie never told Brooke how he felt, and there was only one other person in the world that knew his true feelings toward her.

Brooke and Scottie exchanged banter for a few more minutes and then finalized the plans that they came to put in motion.

Chapter 2
Digging In

Aubrey sat up straight, her long hair falling to the right side of her body. Downtown Philadelphia was beautiful, and the pure white snow that lay on the architectural beauties was intriguing. As Aubrey admired the historical downtown Philly, the cab slowed down.

"Miss, we're here," the cab driver announced with a big grin, trying to redeem himself.

Aubrey smiled as she exited the cab. The driver motioned for her to go ahead and said he would bring her bags in. When Aubrey turned to face the massive front doors of the Ritz Carlton, the bellboys swooped down on the cab driver and stripped him of his potential tip. Aubrey paid her fare and left the cab driver standing there with the exact change.

Aubrey chuckled as she strutted into the plush layout of the upscale hotel. She almost missed the beauty and uniqueness of her destination fooling with the rude cab driver. As she lifted her head from laughter, air escaped her lungs and her body struggled to replace the oxygen as she inhaled. The Ritz Carlton was gorgeous. The entrance, which was supported by two pure marble pillars, gave the hotel the appearance of a historic museum.

While admiring the vibrant, elegant decor throughout the lobby and the glass staircase in the center of the lobby, Aubrey reached the front desk. The receptionist was even high-class, wearing a tailored charcoal Chanel blazer, black pencil skirt, and black suede pumps. Standing behind the desk, she gave Aubrey a bright, pleasant smile.

"Welcome to the Ritz Carlton. How may I serve you?"

Aubrey cleared her throat and proudly announced, "I have a penthouse reservation for Aubrey Green. I called ahead."

After checking her computer, the lady asked Aubrey for ID and method of payment. Providing the required items to complete her check-in, Aubrey was on her way to her new home for the time being. Aubrey strutted toward the elevator feeling important and respected. Those two things were all she desired in the world, and when she did not get them, she became dangerous.

As Aubrey passed the bar area of the hotel, she noticed a sexy guy sitting alone having a drink. He caught eyes with her and did a double take. She smiled at him, and he watched her walk away. The elevator arrived, and the bellboys hurried on with her bags. Aubrey put her key in and turned it to unlock the elevator bound for the penthouse.

Justin sat at the round marble table finishing his drink. He had the mystery woman on his mind and was determine to find out who she was. Justin was usually not the kind of guy to chase strange women, but something was pulling him toward Aubrey, and he had no idea why.

Justin Webber was a thirty-two-year-old, single, successful businessman and a bi-racial stud. A native of the great city of Philadelphia, he enjoyed the downtown life. Justin was one of the executives at The Ritz Carlton, and he loved his job so much that he hung around even on his days off.

Justin walked toward the front of the lobby, greeting guests with a smile and a hello as he approached his destination. The front desk receptionist fixed her clothing and stood up straight at the sight of Justin. His presence made her nervous--partly because he was so sexy and partly because he was very stern and particular about the running of the hotel.

"Hello, Mr. Webber," she said in a shaky voice, trying to control her breathing.

Justin said his greetings without making eye contact. He cleared the computer screen with the touch of a button and then typed in his password. Justin was on a mission and not interested in small talk. Justin looked up the information for the penthouse guest, and his eyes lit up when he discovered that Aubrey had put up a cash deposit for the suite.

What do you do, Ms. Green, to be able to afford $4,000 a night plus deposit? Justin thought to himself before logging off and preparing his mind for his hot pursuit.

* * * * *

Aubrey arrived at her lavish abode. The double doors to the suite were the gate to an oasis in the sky. She entered with expectations of the "wow factor", and that is just what she received. Aubrey stood in the center of the massive living room and was consumed by the panoramic view of downtown Philadelphia.

"Wow," she said, then let out a long sigh.

Despite her lavish surroundings and the extra money Aubrey possessed, it didn't soothe her feelings of sorrow. She had left everything behind and was determined to meet her goals, but it was lonely starting over.

Wanting to get settled in, Aubrey put her clothes away in the huge walk-in closet. She stepped back and was disgusted.

"Damn, I need to go shopping. This closet swallows up my clothes."

She tucked her bags of money away and then prepared to set up a list of things to do, but first, she was in desperate need of a long, hot bath. She exited the closet adjacent to the master bathroom and started her bath water. Spotting the fireplace anchored in the right corner of the bathroom, she placed five logs inside and added fire. Finally, her body began to warm up, and she slipped into her hot bath.

Aubrey attempted to relax, but it was hard to do with her mind on the list she needed to create. In spite of her mind fighting her body, she placed her head on the ledge of the oversized tub, took a few deep breaths, and closed her eyes. Her mind aligned with her body, and she inhaled the sweet smell of the Jasmine bubble bath.

* * * * *

Justin wracked his brain trying to figure out what would be a good excuse to run into Aubrey. What will I say? How will I approach her and where? All of these questions ran through his mind. What would be the right gift to bring? His mother instructed him as a young boy to always bring a lady a negotiating gift when attempting to get to know her better, and he planned to do just that. Only thing was he didn't know what

Aubrey liked. Justin went into deep-thinking mode; he had to see her exotic beauty once again.

* * * * *

Aubrey finished with her wonderful soak. Her body still warmed from the outside in, she sat on the king-sized bed with her paper and pen in hand. She began jotting down the next moves she would need to make in order to get comfortable in the new city.

1. Find permanent housing
2. Buy a car
3. Go shopping for new clothes
4. Locate publishers in the city

She stopped at four and crossed it out, replacing it with...

4. Research self-publishing/starting own publishing house
5. Find a man

Aubrey stopped as she felt a weight of sadness come over her. She had dreamed of being a writer since she was young, but she knew she would not do very well working under anyone. She did not take orders at all. She also knew that finding a man should not have even been on her list. She was supposed to be starting new and holding her own. Her sadness turned into rage.

"I hate you bitch!" she yelled. "You're a piece of shit! Look what I have become because of you. Throwing my talent down the drain and following in your footsteps got me in the situation that I'm in!"

Aubrey yelled at the ceiling as if it were a person. She treated it like the person she hated more than her dead oppressor Jerome; her mother, Cynthia. She hated the fact that her mother was a whore and had always put men over her. She never told Aubrey much about her father. Aubrey believed she probably did not know who her father was.

Cynthia used her looks to get what she wanted, and the last man she sunk her teeth into married her and took her away. She was never to be seen again. Over the years, not even a raggedy card was sent to Aubrey, who was raised by her grandmother.

Aubrey trembled, and the tears that filled her eyes spilled over liked a boiling pot of water. She sobbed loudly at first, and then her cries were muffled as she buried her face in the pillow. Aubrey's long, curly hair hung over the side of the bed as she attempted to pace her breathing before passing out. She lay naked, weeping all alone. Thoughts of her murdering spree raced through her head, driving her further into depression. Aubrey fought hard to be free from the oppression of Jerome, but now that she was free, she felt like she did not have any other place in the world to go. Her writing used to be her refuge, but since her last day in Atlanta, she struggled to produce anything of substance. Her last story written was completed and ready to shop around; but she was reluctant to put it out in the world.

Aubrey pulled herself up out of bed and headed toward the bathroom to wash her face with a cold rag. As she approached the sink, she heard a knock at the door. Aubrey was startled at first, but figured it was the hotel bellboy checking to see if she needed anything. She did not know anyone in the city yet, and besides, the penthouse had its own key slot in the elevator. Therefore, the suite was not accessible to just anyone.

She located the plush white robe with the gold symbol in the left corner.

"Just a minute!" Aubrey yelled out.

She hurried to the door, hoping it was the help so she could place an order for the grocery service and private car service for a few days. Aubrey opened one side of the door enough to see out in the hallway, while half of her body remained behind the door. There stood the sexy man from the bar dressed in a tailor-fitted all black suit, ivory pinstriped shirt, and canary yellow tie.

"Yes," she said in her country drawl. She was not at all prepared for a visitor.

Justin perused her beautiful body, or at least what the half-opened robe exposed. Aubrey clutched her robe tight when she saw the look on his face, not knowing if she should get her gat or call the front desk for help about the stalker at her door. Aubrey started in when Justin did not answer right away.

"How tha' hell you get up here?"

Justin snapped out of his trance when he realized Aubrey was very upset. "Ms. Green, I am Justin Webber, and this is my hotel. I came up here to personally welcome you to The Ritz Carlton."

He pulled his hand from behind his back and presented Aubrey with a dozen of red and black roses. Immediately, Aubrey's behavior changed to sultry, more so because he told her it was his hotel and not so much because of the roses. She could taste money, and it turned her into whatever was needed to be to obtain it. That was a gift she had learned from her days as a dancer in the strip club; be whatever fantasy to get what she wanted. Aubrey had plenty of money in the bank and stuffed in her closet; but the more, the better was her motto. Noticing she had relaxed a little, Justin took the opportunity to swoop down.

"Ms. Green--"

She interrupted his speech. "Please, call me Aubrey. I've never been personally welcomed in any hotel before," she said with a seductive grin.

Justin countered, "And I've never had my breath stolen by such a beautiful guest before. Here are two tickets to the orchestra at the Kimmel Center. You and a guest can enjoy an evening out on me."

Aubrey's sugar walls pulsated. It was nothing like a sexy, powerful man with money...complete turn-on. Aubrey accepted the gift and thanked Justin. Just as she turned to walk away, she let her robe fall open; giving him a brief peep at what she was working with.

Chapter 3
Southern Discomfort

The lights flashed and the air was full of show smoke. Men were wall to wall in the popular strip club. The Mouse Trap housed some of the most beautiful women in the south. Girls came from all over to work the platinum stage of Jerome Kobbs. He kept balling clientele that loved to spend money. Even though he loved to take credit for the club's success, the girls made the business run without any effort. There were women of all shapes and sizes that were the best in their class.

This night was no different as far as the stripper's work ethic. The dressing room was on fire with ambition. Beautiful outfits and jeweled footwear was the standard uniform, although they did not stay dressed for long. Seductress after seductress graced the stage and kept the crowd satisfied. The night was winding down, and even though the Mouse Trap was lively and full of beauties, a couple of strippers were missing due to an outbreak of the flu. So, the acts went a little longer to make up the difference. One thing all of Jerome's strippers knew is that he did not play when it came to his money. He usually came out during the last act to be sure they all were working hard to get as much money as possible before they closed.

This particular night, the headliner, Breeze, was not present, which meant next in line was Spice, a six-foot, curvaceous and exotic amazon from Brazil. The lights dimmed, and the music played on cue. As R. Kelly sang "Move your body like a snake, ma," Spice slid down the silver pole center stage and came out of her sheer Jeanie outfit in a seductive manner. As she stood wearing nothing but a diamond thong, the crowd yelled for more. She stuck her left leg out, exposing the large tattoo of a colorful snake that was wrapped around her thigh, with the snake's head resting near her panty line. Spice moved her body in a slow snake-like motion as she spread her legs, going all the way down to the stage floor. Spice straddled a black basket, and out came a black snake that hissed and moved in unison with her. The crowd went wild, and money fell from the sky like steady rain.

Inside the dressing room, the chatter was loud and the movement whirled throughout. Everyone was talking about how much money they had made, and jokes about whose goodies were worth more and whose was on food stamps continued between laughter and the discussion of plans for the night.

When Spice entered the dressing room with her pet snake, applauds were all around. Spice noticed she had not seen Jerome the entire night. Jerome sometimes stayed in his office while he watched the activities on his many cameras, but it was not like him not to show up for the last call.

Curious about the absence of Jerome, Spice quickly cleaned up and headed for his office. She walked down the narrow hallway and anticipated finding Jerome held up in his space getting sucked off by the new girl. As she approached the office door, she spotted Big Thor standing at his normal post, but something was different. Jerome's light was off in his office, and Thor reported he had not seen him, but he was at his post just in case he showed up.

Spice walked away, shaking her head and laughing under her breath. How did a fat country boy get so much power? After counting her earnings, she headed out of the club.

Spice drove through the streets of Atlanta with her window cracked, trying to stay awake. It was three o'clock in the morning, and she was in need of her usual late-night fix. Spice attempted to call her "sponsor" several times, but received no answer. In desperate need of some good head and a little extra money, Spice decided to go to his house and give him a little booty-call surprise.

She turned her music down when she turned onto the suburban street. Pulling her Tahoe into her usual parking spot, she quickly looked in her rearview mirror as she rubbed her fingers through her thick, dark brown hair. Daddy, here I come. Hope you're ready to taste this all night.

The six-inch heels on her boots echoed off of the ground, and mounds of snow outlined the edges of the parking lot. She was careful not to step in any snow and risk being out of work for any number of days.

It was Sunday morning now, and most of the houses were occupied. The norm for the area was to go out early Saturday night, get wasted, and return home about two or three o'clock on Sunday morning to prepare for another week. Spice knew this all too well, because a few times when she was receiving the great headjob that he put on her, no neighbors were even home to hear her loud screams of pleasure.

Spice reached the front door and rang the bell. She could see the lights on and hear music playing low in the background. Next, Spice called his phone and leaned her body against the door, placing her ear against it to determine if she heard a ring from inside. She fell in the door headfirst, as her purse and its belongings went everywhere. The halfway shut door was a little less than sturdy.

The site that greeted Spice was unbelievable. Jerome's nude body was right by the door in the living room, and Quanda's naked body was further inside the house by the entrance to the hallway. Spice let out a scream that could wake the dead. She clawed the floor, pushing her body up, and then ran out of the house so fast that she broke her heel. Spice jumped in her car and sped off with tires screeching and smoking.

Lights flashed throughout the beautiful urban street. The neighbors were now awake and standing on their lawn in various quantities. They never had so much police presence in the neighborhood before this night. No words were being exchanged between the police and the curious neighbors. Despite the cold air and blizzard-like snow, people poured out of their houses to see the reason for the commotion. The news vans were on site, which meant something serious had gone down.

Detective Torrey arrived after being called by the first officers on the scene. They drove up to the house expecting for it to be a domestic dispute or some lockout situation. From the report of the neighbor that called, it was as if loud noise was a disturbance. When the two officers entered the house, they were not prepared for what they saw.

Detective Torrey approached the tall officer that was obviously in charge, while the officer's partner puked in the bushes.

Looking down at the officer who was hunched over, Detective Torrey said, "Damn rookie."

The officer standing extended his hand and said, "Officer Deville, and yes, he's a rookie. We were first on the scene for what we thought was an ordinary disturbance call, but what we discovered was anything but. We found two bodies, one by the front door and the other body at the entrance to the hallway. Not looking good at all."

Officer Torrey stood taking in the perfectly depicted scene. He waited for the perfect opportunity to begin his questioning and further investigation.

Scratching his head, he took a deep breath and asked, "Did your officers comb the crime scene thoroughly and the immediate area all the way to the parking lot? We can't let anything get away from us."

Officer Deville took a deep breath, as well, before replying, "Already on it. The evidence is in sealed bags. We found several items that look like contents out of a purse. There was also a heel from someone's shoe. The search was a good one."

"I'll see about that. I like to handle my own scenes, as I'm sure you were probably already told. The smallest thing can be the largest asset to cracking a case. That's how it's done where I come from," Detective Torrey stated with an arrogant tone.

Ellis Torrey was one of the best in his class, having a ninety percent accuracy rate with cracking all of the cases he was assigned. He had just been recruited from New York City and missed the action he was used to on the job. With his wife getting a position at a local hospital in Atlanta as the director of psychology, he felt it was a good move to make.

Detective Torrey was a dying breed; a clean cop that actually did his job and did it well. He was raised in

31

Philadelphia until the age of eighteen when he went away to college. The University of New York was where he started his college career in sports therapy. He soon discovered his love for psychology after taking criminology for an elective because all of the easy classes were full. He earned an "A" in the class and was hooked from there. Detective Torrey still had his mind set on being a sports therapist and owning a business, until he met the prettiest and smartest girl on campus, who asked him the question that changed his life and made him think about things in a different way.

Detective Torrey was doing his usual thing chasing skirts as he attempted to get to know Julecia Banks. He told her stories about being the guy that professional athletes could count on. Being insightful as she was, Julecia could tell the dream that Ellis bragged about was not his own. She knew someone that absorbed the law and information about the minds of criminals in their psychology classes had to have a passion for the field of psychology.

Julecia sat at the round table in the left corner of the cafeteria at University of New York listening to Ellis go on and on, while looking very pleased with himself as he tried hard to impress her. Julecia moved close enough to him that she could have kissed him, full tongue and everything. Ellis perked up at the thought of the beauty making the first move.

He braced himself for the encounter, but instead of his anticipated physical exchange, Julecia placed her right hand on his cheek and said, "Why do you continue to spew this rehearsed fantasy? You are an excellent criminologist that will soar above the expectations of many. Stop being who you think people want you to be and just do what comes natural. You will then live a life fulfilled and make a difference."

Those words stayed with him and so did Julecia Banks, who eventually became Julecia Torrey.

Chapter 4
Caged Bird

Center stage, the lights danced over Spice's body like diamonds. She had the crowd going wild. Men attempted to climb on the stage as she brought them to fireballs of desire. Spice was in a zone. Her peers were even mesmerized by the way her body moved as if she had no bones. Something was different about her, but they could not put their finger on it. She was more daring.

Spice bent over, her bottom facing the crowd as she slipped off her jeweled body jewelry and G-string. In one motion, she spun around moving to the beat She got a donk, she got a donk. She gyrated, giving the crowd a full frontal of absolute nudity. Her perfectly trimmed vagina glistened with glitter. The money rained down like a Tsunami. The DJ took her cue and switched up with a mix leading into "I'm In Love with a Stripper".

She rocks it, she rolls it... From the stage, Spice made love to every man and woman in the building, sliding up and down on the pole as she rubbed the money all over her naked body. Her set lasted about twenty minutes longer than usual, and nobody complained except her competition. She had a line of dudes waiting for a lap dance as she strutted past them, not even covering up as she had done in the past. The girls were surprised to see her in that light. Everyone knew she was Jerome's main girl and the only one that actually enjoyed being with him. She also was not allowed to ever get fully nude.

Headed directly for the bathroom, she whisked past everyone in the dressing room. The girls called out to her with fake cheers as the bathroom door shut loudly; she knew they were salty about her performance. Spice sat on the edge of the toilet and broke down in tears. Her high was coming down, and she felt the pain of what she had seen not even twenty-four hours ago.

Bang! Bang! Bang! The knocks on the door startled her.

"I'll be out in a minute," Spice said in between sniffles.

There was silence at the door before it was pushed open. There Spice sat now on the floor of the bathroom, bent over sniffing hefty lines of coke. Bliss stood there in shock.

"Spice, what the fuck are you doing?"

Bliss was one of the girls at the club who was friendly with Spice outside of work and truly cared about her wellbeing. Spice just broke down crying and attempted to speak in between sobs.

Spice had fallen for Jerome years ago when he got her out of an abusive relationship, helped her get clean, and gave her a job. Born Cindy Dorsey in Brazil and raised in Chicago, Illinois she saw life through both of her parent's culture. Spice traveled to Atlanta to start a life with her high school sweetheart, who turned out to be a monster that got her hooked on coke and would beat her ass whenever he felt like it.

Jerome met her when she tried to pick him up for a trick. Instead, he saw potential in her to make him some money. He picked her up and helped her get on her feet. From there, Spice was born, but she and Jerome kept a special connection. Not the traditional husband and wife monogamous relationship, but a connection nonetheless.

Bliss attempted to close the bathroom door to avoid the spectacle and litany of gossip. The dressing room suddenly became a horror flick. There was a loud boom and then a crash. After the loud crash, Spice and Bliss could hear screams throughout the dressing room. Over the screams, they heard the loud voices of men shouting, "Get down and don't move!"

Police officers were everywhere. Accompanied by Detective Torrey, who was waving a paper in his hand, they entered the club from the front and back doors.

"We have a search warrant. No one can leave the premises until we're done," Detective Torrey told them.

As Spice began to panic, Bliss did not know what had gotten into her. Spice jumped up, attempting to claw her way out of the small window in the bathroom.

"What are you doing, girl!" Bliss yelled. "Your ass is naked. Spice, talk to me. Are you in trouble?" Bliss didn't know how much trouble Spice was really in.

Detective Torrey heard the crash coming from the bathroom and quickly ran to locate the noise. There Spice was attempting to escape through the window, coke on the floor, and Bliss standing in the middle of the floor with tears flowing down her face. After helping a hysterical Spice down, Detective Torrey escorted her and Bliss to the station. He had a hunch he had struck gold, but he knew if nothing else, he could hold her on a drug charge while he continued his investigation.

CHAPTER 5

Hidden Pleasure

The sound coming from the headboard was enough to excite a nun. The frame of Brenson's king-size cherry wood bed rattled to the rhythmic beat of the body orchestra. He rocked his hips slowly as if it was the last time he would experience her body. His bedroom was the pleasure zone, and he was the conductor. The oversized window anchored in the wall took up seventy-five percent of the space. Light streamed in through the window, illuminating his lover's body like a show light. The spacious bedroom set fit perfectly in his stylish downtown condo.

She moaned and breathed deep, taking all he had to offer. To him, this was the closest thing to heaven that he would ever experience. Brooke had never had her pipes cleaned like Brenson cleaned them. Each stroke had meaning, and his body and mind was on one frequency. Everything he felt and thought was put into pleasuring her.

Brooke looked up at his sexy, chiseled body as Maxwell played in the background. Brenson's feet were planted on the bed, and he had both of her legs on his shoulders as he gave it to her leapfrog style. Each bounce of the bed gave her double pleasure, as his member hit the top and bottom of her walls with precision.

"Oh shit, Bren, I'm almost there. This issssss...ooooohhhh my goodness."

Brenson's stroking had Brooke unable to finish her sentence.

"This is all yours. I'm comin', baby!"

Brenson quickened his stroke, and they screamed in unison, "AHHHHHHH Shiiiit."

They both rolled over, exhausted from their love-fest. Brooke struggled to catch her breath as she opened her eyes to regain her center. The big red numbers on the clock read 12:45. Their morning quickie had turned into a full session. Now they both were late for business meetings, but they had no regrets as they raced to the shower to prepare for their day.

Brenson stood six-feet, one inch and always had a look on his face like he was thinking of his next move. A pecan tan complexion, he had a set of the most alluring hazel eyes. Brenson was not always as successful as he had become in the past six years. He grew up on the north side in a one-bedroom hole-in-the-wall with his mother, who did the best she could to keep a roof over their heads. Brenson's mother was a Spanish beauty who had him at a young age and struggled with his care due to his father being married and unavailable. A young Brenson vowed he would make something of his life and help his mother out of the ghetto.

Brenson had done a good job with keeping his focus and working toward his dreams. He always did well in school, and he practically raised himself because his mother acted more like a sister to him than a parent. By the time he turned fourteen, Brenson was curious to know more about his dad. Outside of the stories his mother had told him, all he had was a name and possible area that he lived in. Determined to find him, Brenson hopped on Septa and headed to his destination. He was amazed at how the neighborhoods changed the further he got out of the hood.

Brenson reached his stop and exited the bus reluctantly. He had no plan and was growing more fearful as he walked through the neighborhood. He saw kids playing and riding the latest Huffy and Mongoose bikes. A sense of sadness mixed with anger came over him all at once. He used to think the reason his father didn't come to see him when he was a little boy was because he was being held against his will and could not break free.

Brenson saw some boys playing in their front yard and politely asked them if they knew Mr. Scotdale Boyd and where he lived. The boys looked at him like he was crazy. They knew a Mr. Boyd, but had no clue who the hell was Scotdale. They laughed at the name and pointed him to the direction of the Boyd family. Brenson walked over to the home, sweating like he had just run a round of roughhouse ball. He looked up at the address and saw that he was in the right place. The street was lined with pretty trees, and the row homes looked different than where he lived. In the badlands of North Philly, or Spanish land 2nd and American Streets, the blocks were small and the houses were close together.

A tall, pretty woman was outside planting flowers in front of the house. Brenson swallowed and approached her.

The woman looked up and said, "Hello. May I help you? If you're looking for one of the boys, they are doing their Saturday chores."

Brenson looked a little confused as he thought to himself, What boys?

Brenson paused and took a deep breath. "I'm here to see Mr. Scotdale Boyd."

Mrs. Boyd became concerned; she didn't know how a young teen would know her husband's whole name.

"Who are you, and why do you need to see my husband?" she asked after standing up.

Brenson couldn't back down; he had come so far. "I'm his son, and I really need to see him."

Mrs. Boyd tripped over the rake that lay on the ground next to her flowerbed. She let out a loud scream as she attempted to regain her footing. Her attempts were unsuccessful as she fell to the ground and hit her head on the sidewalk. The front door swung open, and there stood a tall handsome man calling the name Lilly. Brenson and the man caught eyes, and it seemed as if time stood still. Brenson had thought about this moment for years. Mr. Boyd was looking into a mirror as his bastard child stared at him. He could not say a word.

Scottie ran out of the door behind his dad, and all he could see was his mother on the ground crying and an unfamiliar boy standing over her. He immediately lunged at Brenson, landing a punch to his left cheek. Scottie then picked up the rake and swung it wildly, almost cracking Brenson in the head. Brenson tried to side step the blow, but fell to the ground.

Mr. Boyd attempted to help his wife up as he gave Scottie verbal prompts to stop. Sixteen years old and full of testosterone, Scottie refused to back down. He jumped on top of Brenson and pressed the handle of the rake against his throat.

With tears in his eyes, Brenson mustered up enough strength to say, "Daddy, please help me."

Scottie stopped and looked at his dad with tear-stained eyes, then looked back at Brenson. The teenager that he thought was a thug attempting to rob his mother was actually his dad's illegitimate love child. Scottie jumped up off of Brenson and took off running. He had so many emotions and questions in his head that he could not deal with at the moment. Brenson did not get the welcome reception he had hoped for. Instead, he was beaten and received no words from his dad.

Fresh out of the shower, Brenson and Brooke were trying to keep their hands off of each other. Brooke adorned her frame with a one-piece all black Gucci bodysuit, black blazer, and red crocodile belt. Brenson was still drying off, and Brooke was ready for her afternoon meeting with the caterers and venue manager for the "Bossin' Up" Ball.

Buzzzzzz! Buzzzzzz! The doorbell sounded as the person leaned on the button.

Brooke looked at Brenson with a funny look and asked, "You expecting someone?"

Brenson returned her a funny look and responded, "Hell no. I was supposed to meet Scottie for a business lunch, but not here."

Brooke had a look of terror on her face. "Are you serious? Do you think it's him?"

"I don't know, but if it is, he cannot see you...us here together!"

They both had agreed that their relationship was not good for Scottie to know about. The problem was they both had their reasons why they felt Scottie should not know about them. Brooke was under the impression that Brenson had her best interest at heart, but the truth is that he was totally selfish in his actions. Scottie and he had become close after that day of their emotional run-in. So close that Scottie and Brenson were inseparable, and Scottie confided in him about mostly everything, even the fact that he had been secretly in love with Brooke since college and someday wanted to be with her.

Scottie returned home late that night after wandering the neighborhood aimlessly, angry with his father and confused as to how he could have a younger brother when his parents had been married for years. After the incident, he overheard his parents discussing Brenson and his living arrangements countless times. He hated that his father had ruined their perfect family and did not understand why he would father a child outside of his marriage and then leave that child in the slums while he lived a middle-class life or what was known as living "hood rich". Scottie's title of being the baby of the family was changed in the blink of an eye and he hated it.

It wasn't until Brenson's mother passed from a heroin overdose that he got to experience the same life that Scottie experienced. From age sixteen (Brenson) and eighteen (Scottie), they shared everything under the same roof.

Brenson went to the intercom, while Brooke stared at the clock and clutched her purse against her stomach, hoping their assumptions were wrong.

Brenson spoke into the intercom. "Who is it?"

There was a pause, and he thought the visitor had left. But then, there were three thumps at the door, and they both almost jumped out of their skin.

"Yo, dude, you in there? Open the damn door."

Brenson gave Brooke the signal to be quiet.

"Who is it?" Brenson said again.

"Dude, you know who the hell it is. Open the door!"

Brenson cracked open the door just enough for Scottie to know he wasn't dressed.

"What's up? You had me waiting for your ass for about an hour. Remember our lunch meeting for today? I have lots to talk about, and you better have some information on all my millions!"

Both men laughed. Brenson cleared his throat, and Brooke stepped back, knocking over a vase on the table in the foyer.

"Dammit," Brooke uttered softly, trying not to be heard.

"Give me a half hour, man, and I'll meet you at the spot." Brenson paused to glance behind him before adding, "I'm kind of tied up in here."

Scottie paused when he heard the whispered voice of a female. "Damn, homey, since when do you blow off business for some female? Hurry ya ass up, and not a moment over thirty minutes or ya ass is FIRED!"

Brenson cracked a half smile and responded, "Got you. Thirty minutes."

While walking away, Scottie mumbled to himself, "Family and business don't mix."

Chapter 6
The Pursuit of It All

The day was off to a good start. Aubrey rolled over and noticed the gloomy weather had gone, and although the air in Philadelphia could feel like razor blades against flesh, Aubrey was just happy it was no longer snowing and raining. The sun was out, and from her window, the scenery was picture perfect.

Aubrey pulled the sheer curtains back and took a deep breath. She had been in Philly for a few weeks and was excited to be downtown where all the action was. Gift shops, eateries, and much more kept Aubrey busy throughout the day and night. Today was a different day, though. It was the day her plan would come together to get Justin on her team and to get in his pockets.

She grabbed her pad from by the bed and glanced at her to-do list. She had shopped for clothes, searched for houses online, and after having decided to shop her script titled Southern Sassy around, she did a little research on the publishing houses in the city. Aubrey was eager to see if going with a large publishing house would benefit her more than trying to start her own company, especially without having any experience and connections in the town. Her next task was to find a residence and lay low while continuing to write, but not before hooking Justin and using his resources to further her growth. Aubrey decided to stay at the hotel for a little   longer.

Aubrey purposely did not contact Justin since their last encounter. She was a master of illusion when it came to men. This was something she mastered long ago in the strip joint. Aubrey was good at becoming whatever men needed to get in their pockets. She did not answer her phone or return his calls as not to seem too easy. But, it was time for her to set the stage. Aubrey picked up the tickets Justin had given her and planted a kiss on them.

"Time for action!" she said aloud.

Aubrey cleared her throat and dialed zero on the telephone.

"Thanks for calling guest services at The Ritz. How may I serve you?"

Aubrey was silent until the representative finished her introduction. "Yes, I'm looking for Mr. Justin Webber. Is he available?"

"Is there something I can help you with? Do you have a problem, ma'am? I will be more than happy to help you."

Aubrey sighed. "Well, if Justin is not available, I will just speak to him when he is and inform him that you were too busy to get him to the phone for me, even though there is a problem in the penthouse."

With her plan in motion, Aubrey hung up the phone and headed for the shower.

* * * * *

Brooke drove down the expressway coming from her business meeting, reminiscing about the session her and Brenson had a few days prior. She was sprung over the love stick and could not get him out of her mind. Her feelings for Scottie had always been under control, but she could not hide them much longer. She told herself that they could never be, but if that were true, why was she hiding her and Brenson's fling? She went over it in her mind, trying to rationalize her reasons for hiding her affair from her "friend" Scottie. She had to admit to herself that Brenson and her was not kicking it long and was just really sexually compatible. Still, she could not get him out of her mind. The fact also remained that she was feeling Scottie, too, and not just for his gorgeous chocolate body. She actually felt connected to him, but Brenson took her body to places it had never been.

Their fling started a few months prior after a big event when her tire blew out and Scottie was too plastered to take her home. Brenson had always seemed to favor her, and like most things that Scottie held dear, he somehow wanted to be a part of it.

Brooke drove like a bat out of hell as she sang along to Jennifer Hudson's song. If this isn't love, then what is it? I must be dreaming or just plain crazzzzzy! Brooke tried to hit the high note as she always did, but falling short, as usual. Her anthem was interrupted by her car phone. When she saw it was Scottie, she got nervous all over again.

"Hello, Brooke speaking."

Scottie laughed as he could not understand why she was trying to be professional when he knew his name and number appeared on her dashboard screen.

"You okay, Brookie? What's with all the formality? Are you actually about to start working for me instead of just saying you do?" Scottie laughed, and that put her at ease.

She was still a little uneasy, but she loosened up a little, trying to sound normal with him.

"Big head, you can't live without me, so stop frontin'! I'm on my way to you as we speak."

"Keep telling yourself that shit and you just may believe it. See you in a little bit, hopefully with a full report about this "Bossin' Up" Ball. I talked to Brenson, and I need to really keep an eye on the financial end of this event."

The mention of Brenson's name made her feel like she was standing in front of Scottie ass naked...real transparent. She began to stumble over her words.

"Ooh...umm...yeah...how is he doing?"

"Girl, stop doing drugs. Remember, puff, puff pass. Stop hogging that shit! You all tongue tied. What's that about? Ask him when you get here. He's coming, too. I just called him because I think he needs to be in on this meeting since he's the financial advisor of my enterprise. See you when you get here...oh, and hurry yo' ass up!"

Brooke hung up and tried to get her thoughts together before entering the meeting. She was not even there yet, but felt as if she was sitting on sharp needles.

* * * * *

Aubrey stepped out of the shower, and the steam filled the air. As she bent down to towel dry her long tresses, she heard the doorbell ring. She went into instant Bre mode. Getting into character, Aubrey wiggled to the front door, wearing nothing but a towel. When she opened the door, Justin's eyes told the story.

"Hello, Ms. Green. I got a call telling me that you had a problem up here."

Aubrey stepped to the side and gave him a devilish grin. "Do you always make house calls for your customers?"

They stared at each other, increasing the sexual tension that was obvious.

"Well, when my favorite customer calls with a problem, I come personally to handle it."

Aubrey smiled and said, "Well, come in, Mr. Fix It. Let me show you the problem."

As she led him to the bathroom, Justin did not know what to think. He was not prepared for a quickie.

"My showerhead would not change settings, and I was stuck with one setting ... faaaaasssssst, and I like it slow sometimes."

With Aubrey making things hot as lava, Justin almost fell into the tub. He checked her shower, and the smell of her sweet jasmine body butter drove him crazy.

"Well, your shower should work fine now. The head just needed tightening up. I see you are preparing for your day, so I'll see you next time you have a problem," Justin said, then proceeded to walk toward the door. However, he did not want to leave without making his move. So, he turned and said, "Since you are paying for a five-star penthouse and you had some issues, I'll give you a night free, but you have to let me take you to breakfast. I can have the chef prepare a private meal of your choice, and you can't say no. Just tell me when you'll be ready, and I'll meet you in the lobby."

Smiling, Aubrey responded, "As tempting as it sounds, I need to get ready to go house hunting, and breakfast would just put me back a few hours."

Aubrey was testing him. She knew if he really was trying to get with her, he would offer to take her, and then she could see what type of wheels he was rolling on.

Just as she had planned, Justin blurted out, "Well, the least I can do is show you around my beautiful city. I know the best kept neighborhoods."

"That sounds good, Mr. Webber, but you're working, and I would like to get an early start. What time do you get off?"

"What time do you need to go?" Justin inquired.

Aubrey smiled at his persistence. "In about an hour."

"I will pick you up in front of the building, and just because I like you, I will call my premium realtor to assist us."

"What car am I looking for out front?"

"You won't be able to miss me! See you in sixty minutes, Ms. Green."

Aubrey rubbed her hands down her towel and replied, "You can call me Bre, and I'll see you in fifty-nine minutes."

* * * * *

Scottie sat quietly pondering what had gotten into Brooke. He was not sure why, but she had been acting strange the past few weeks.

"Maybe it's the upcoming ball...too much pressure," Scottie said out loud, before looking down at his watch to make sure of the time. "Damn, is everyone running late?" He let out a sigh.

Just then, Scottie felt a firm squeeze on his right shoulder. As he turned, he was met with a bright smile.

"Bro, you sitting here talking to yourself? Now that's real bad. Sorry I'm late. Traffic is a bitch out there!"

Scottie paused and returned the warm salutations.

"Hey, bro! I was just wondering why all my important business colleagues are late, including you. As I always say, time is money and money is time!"

Brenson had heard this speech all too many times and could use a break from it. "I hear you, bro, and I apologize once again."

Brenson hated when Scottie pulled rank, even if what he was saying was true. He had lived in Scottie's shadow for too long and had not grown accustomed to it. The problem is he wanted what Scottie had.

* * * * *

Brooke could not concentrate on her task at hand. She was preoccupied with the news that Brenson would be joining her and Scottie during their meeting. Brooke had not seen Brenson and Scottie together since the party that landed her and Brenson in the bed. She hated that she felt as if she was cheating on Scottie. She was not ready to admit why she wanted to continue to keep her and Brenson a secret.

As she came out of deep thought, Brooke caught a glimpse of her reflection in the rearview mirror and smiled. She had just gotten a fresh manicure and hairdo. She loved her hairdresser Chereé because she would open up her shop at six o'clock in the morning just for Brooke to keep her hair tight.

Brooke pulled up to the restaurant, while slowly gaining her confidence back

"Act normal, Brooke! Business first!" she shouted at her reflection.

The tires of her souped-up Mustang screeched as she raced to get a parking spot closest to the door. The sleek classic beauty purred as the tires fit neatly in the parking space. Brooke chose her cars like she chose her daily fashion. She was in a sexy/sporty mood, and her Mustang represented that.

The Chatué was as lively as she remembered from their last lunch date. She approached the oversized crystal door and took a deep breath before entering.

"Here goes nothing," she whispered.

The upscale restaurant was decorated to perfection with sexy black and white prints that graced the walls. The high ceilings and exposed wood beams housed decorative lighting, while splashes of color were strategically placed throughout the space inside. Brooke spotted Scottie, Brenson, and an unidentified woman sitting in the left corner of the restaurant. As she approached the table, Scottie spotted her and waved.

"Hey, Brooke. You decided to join us," he said with his usual sarcastic grin.

Brooke gave him a half smile. She was too busy staring at Brenson and the woman laughing and engrossed in conversation.

Scottie looked surprised. "What, no comeback? Just a smile?"

Brooke cleared her throat and replied, "Good afternoon, everyone."

Scottie and Brenson looked at her with confusion. Brooke's lack of engagement was unfamiliar.

Across Town...

Aubrey strutted to the private elevator with confidence. She could not wait to spend more time with Justin. He was sexy and gorgeous, but most of all, she could smell the money dripping from his tailored suit. Their initial encounter was not as fruitful due to her not knowing she was staying in his hotel, as he had referred to it. She was excited to hit the jackpot so soon after arriving in Philadelphia.

The elevator doors opened, and she was taken to the center of the stylish upscale lobby of The Ritz Carlton, which reminded her that she was living in luxury and needed to stop worrying about her past. Aubrey's six-inch red-bottoms clicked against the floor with each step.

Stopping to take in all the scenery, she whispered, "I can get used to this."

As she approached the oversized front entrance, she spotted Justin standing out front with his back toward the hotel and looking down at his watch. She paused, wanting to make him wait a little longer.

"Ma'am, may I help you?" a concerned hotel employee inquired.

In a tone of annoyance, Aubrey replied, "No, I am just fine."

Aubrey figured she better exit the building before a gang of helpful employees bombarded her. She giggled at her own annoyance with being treated with "five-star" service. Aubrey was not all the way outside, when Justin turned to follow the delicious smell.

"Wow, you look and smell wonderful!"

Justin handed Aubrey a large bouquet of exotic flowers, and she began to flirt instantly.

"Thank you, sir. I hope I'm not overdressed for our outing." She spun around, playfully showing off her beautiful emerald green silk mini-dress accompanied by thigh-high red-bottom boots and a short mink jacket.

He replied, "Not at all. You're dressed just right for any outing."

Justin stood there with his hand outstretched, gesturing for Aubrey to follow his lead. Aubrey grabbed his hand and was escorted to a shiny black Porsche Turbo Cayenne SUV. She was smiling in secret places that could not be seen as the driver got out and opened the door for them. Their trip through the city had begun, and she was happy to be his guest.

The snow that remained was a perfect backdrop and gave the city a cozy, inviting vibe. Aubrey and Justin continued to engage in their flirty banter throughout their drive.

Remembering their conversation from earlier, Aubrey asked, "So when will we actually be meeting your realtor? I really need to find a spot that I can call home, ya know?"

Aubrey's slight southern accent was so sexy to Justin.

"Do you always need to know every move beforehand Ms. Green?"

Aubrey fluttered her eyelashes and replied, "Why, of course. I only like to be blindfolded in private."

They both laughed.

As the driver began to slow down, Aubrey became curious as to where Justin was taking her since she did not see any homes in sight. The car stopped, and then the driver got out and opened their doors.

Justin looked Aubrey in the eyes and said, "Welcome to my favorite place on earth, besides my own kitchen."

Aubrey smiled as they entered the restaurant. The atmosphere was breathtaking.

Aubrey paused before blurting out, "I'll take it! This is absolutely stunning."

Justin smiled at her, feeling proud of his selection in eateries. A tall blonde lady approached them and gave Justin a hug. Aubrey gave Justin a strange look. Justin stepped back after their embrace and turned to face Aubrey.

"Well, I don't think it's for sale, but maybe she can help us find you somewhere that is. Aubrey, meet Lynn Sholtz, realtor extraordinaire!"

Lynn reached out her hand to seal the deal of the introduction.

"Nice to meet you. Can you make this happen?" Aubrey asked playfully.

Lynn smiled and replied, "I can make anything happen but that!"

A male host dressed in all black walked up looking like pure eye-candy. "Right this way, Mr. Webber. Your room is ready."

The host escorted them to a small private room where the table was set for three, and a brunch spread for royalty was on display. Aubrey was definitely impressed, not only with the restaurant, but with Lynn being equipped with house information, blueprints, and stats for each neighborhood.

* * * * *

Scottie was unsure of the intro with Brooke, but he brushed it off to keep the focus of their meeting clear.

"Brooke, this is Amber Delvino, the reporter from The Daily News that wanted to feature me and the company in her write-up about young black entrepreneurs in the city. She will also be interviewing you and Bren as the supporting forces behind my success."

Brooke was so relieved that she threw out an awkward joke. "Well, I'm glad I got my hair did."

They all just looked at her. Her joke was an epic fail. Scottie finally broke the silence.

"Okay, Amber, you got the floor. However you would like to handle the order of your interview and photos is up to you."

Amber started the interview with Scottie. Scottie, Amber, and Brenson discussed the business and "Bossin' Up" event. Brooke was so uncomfortable in the meeting that she could not focus. They discussed the meat of the company and the activities that would take place during the event. Brooke was next up, and feeling the pressure, she excused herself to get a breather before her section and retreated to the restroom.

Bent over and with her arms stretched out Christ-like, she leaned on the restroom mirror. She attempted to slow her breathing and coach herself to calm down. She could not gather her thoughts and did not know what was happening.

"I'm falling apart here. Why?"

Brooke behaved as if she was cheating on Scottie, and it was killing her. She hated keeping secrets; it always made her physically sick. Brooke took one final deep breath, pulled her stomach in, and tossed her hair over her left shoulder. A bright smile came across her face, and she forced herself into character mode. Brooke then swung the restroom doors open dramatically, trying to keep up her confidence. However, she was stopped in her tracks when she saw Brenson standing in front of the restroom. Her confidence along with her perfect posture crumbled.

"What the hell are you standing out here for?"

"Waiting for your crazy ass. What do ya think? Look, you're behaving very oddly, and Scottie is starting to worry. What's up with you? We agreed to keep us a secret due to work issues, right?"

Brenson said his peace in a stern whisper, hoping to find out why Brooke was acting so weird and hoping she would be able to keep them a secret at least for a little while longer.

Brooke retorted, "Look, this is hard for me. Scottie is my good friend and colleague. I hate lying to him, and every time I'm around you two, I think he can see right through us!"

She tried to convince Brenson and herself that the only reason she was acting weird was because she hated hiding them from Scottie, "her friend". Becoming hysterical, Brooke went in on Brenson.

"Why would you come find me? He's not stupid, you know. You should've stayed there until I returned."

Brenson attempted to calm Brooke down before they returned to the table. He reached out to grab her arms that were flailing in the air. "Brooke, get yourself together. He sent me to get you because Amber has another appointment and is ready for you."

Brooke and Scottie tussled in the hallway of the restrooms as he tried to get her calm. They were now blocking the door to the women's restroom. "Excuse me." A woman's voice broke their struggle. Embarrassed, Brooke turned to apologize for blocking the door.

"I'm so sorry, mis--" She stopped in mid-sentence. Her day had just gone from bad to worse.

"BB, is that you?" the woman said. "It's been so long, but you still look the same."

Stunned by her beauty, Brenson found himself lost in her eyes and exotic looks. Aubrey paused for a minute then gave the woman a dry response.

"Hey, Bre, it has been a long time. What are you doing in my city?"

Brooke almost forgot Brenson was standing there until he cleared his throat. Brooke turned to him, forcing herself to appear put together, and said, "Brenson, tell Amber that I will be right there in less than two minutes."

Brenson walked away following orders, but looked back the entire time. Aubrey and Brooke continued their inopportune reunion.

"I just moved to the city," Aubrey told her. "I'm starting fresh; about to go look for a home to plant some roots. Here's my number. Call me. We have to hook up. I know absolutely no one in the city."

Brooke gave her a half smile, wondering when pole-dancing Bre started speaking in that manner.

"Okay, we have to catch up. But, right now, I need to get back to my business meeting."

Aubrey continued to the restroom, while thinking to herself, That shit ain't look like no business to me. We'll see. Aubrey powdered her nose as she thought about her and

Brooke's time in Atlanta. She closed her compact and strutted back to her brunch meeting.

Armed with a great plan of homes to go see, she, Justin, and Lynn were headed out of the restaurant and to Aubrey's new life.

Chapter 7

Calculated Seduction

Aubrey and Justin entered the apartment, and she just knew she was at home. They had seen plenty of houses and apartments, but nothing compared to this one. Lynn, the realtor, began her introduction.

"You are now in the Sterling Apartments located right in the desirable Rittenhouse Square neighborhood."

Aubrey was too preoccupied with the breathtaking view of the city to pay attention to Lynn's spiel.

"Oh, I just love it, Justin! You did good, Lynn."

Justin laughed at her childish enthusiasm. "I'm happy you love it, but you need to take the tour and hear more about it before making your decision."

Lynn chimed in. "I agree, Ms. Green. You need to be comfortable with your decision."

Aubrey stood there pouting. "Okay, let me hear it."

Lynn cleared her throat and continued as just a formality. She knew her commission was in the bag, though.

"The space is 2,350 square feet and is equipped with a washer, dryer, fully-equipped kitchen with granite countertops, four bedrooms, three baths, garage, wall-to-wall plush carpeting, master suite, rooftop pool, full concierge service, and a twenty-four-hour gym."

Lynn went on and on about the place, leaving out the hefty price tag. When Aubrey paused and looked up toward the ceiling, Lynn worried that maybe she was going to change her mind.

"What's wrong, Ms. Green?" Lynn asked.

Aubrey smiled and responded, "I'm just imagining my monogrammed address logo on all of my new stationery. What will my address be?"

Lynn quickly replied, "The address is 1815 John F. Kennedy Boulevard, Philadelphia, Pennsylvania 19103, Apartment---"

Aubrey cut her off. "Price is no object, but what is the asking for my place?'"

Lynn wrote the price down on a piece of paper, and Aubrey jumped for joy. With the money she had cleaned out from Jerome alone, she could pay cash for her place and still have money left over to spare.

"Okay, let's do it. You can get the papers together while Justin and I tour the rest of the apartment."

Aubrey and Justin proceeded to take their tour. Each room was more fabulous than the last. Aubrey had more room than she needed and fantasized about what she would do with each room. Office and sitting room were already chosen in her head.

Justin went through each room unaware that Aubrey had already given him and his money a place in her home and life. She had been taught by the best, and she was not about to let her new sponsor go.

Aubrey and Justin entered the master bedroom, walking slowly to be sure they took it all in. The room was a soft cotton color with textured walls. They had it staged perfectly with a solid hand-carved oak king-size bed anchoring the spacious room. It was complete with a stepstool to use for climbing in the bed and a sea-foam colored silk bed ensemble. A crystal, oversized chandelier hanging by a shimmering chain was positioned above the bed. Pure white carpet kissed each wall, making it feel as if they were walking on clouds. In the corner, there was a white leather wave chair adorned with a fur throw that matched the bedding.

Both Justin and Aubrey were enjoying the view. They walked further back, entering the master bath. Walls were treated with limestone, and the shower was a rendition of an exotic rainforest. Water continuously ran down the stonewall open shower. The shower reflection could be seen in the wall-to-wall mirror. The smell of lavender filled the air, and a gold and white chaise lounge sat in the center of the large master oasis.

Aubrey stood in front of the shower as goose bumps rose all over her body. She inhaled the beautiful aroma, feeling happy for the first time in years. She thought to herself, this just might be for real.

Justin took the opportunity to see how close he could get to Aubrey. The sexual tension between them was obvious, but aside from a little light flirting, he had been a gentleman the entire day. Little did Justin know, Aubrey was creaming over his bankroll; his good looks were just a bonus.

He placed his hand on Aubrey's shoulders, mimicking a massage as leaned in and whispered in her ear, "So how did I do?"

Aubrey arched her back, rubbing her rear against his crotch. Justin was pleasantly surprised. He only expected a hug, maybe a kiss. Aubrey had something else in mind, though. She was used to screwing strangers like she missed them, and Justin was no different. He would be her new sponsor, and it was time to seal the deal.

No more words were exchanged in that moment. Turning to face Justin, Aubrey placed her right index finger over his soft, full lips and followed with a long, sensual kiss. She moved down to his neck, licking in slow, small motions. Justin was not into getting blue balls, but he didn't thinking Aubrey would go all the way with Lynn about four rooms away. However, Aubrey would prove him wrong, and he could do nothing but ride the wave.

Aubrey hiked up her dress, exposing her perfectly round bottom and revealing that the lace stockings were really a one-piece crotchless body stocking. Justin was hard as cement. He grabbed her bottom as he pulled her close to him and kissed her passionately. Aubrey escaped his grasp and slid down seductively to open his trousers with her teeth. She then led him to the chaise, where she sat in front of him with her legs spread eagle. Aubrey flicked her clit as she swallowed his manhood whole. Justin's head fell back as his eyes rolled in the back of his head. Slow, deep moans escaped his lips when he could not hold it any longer. He looked down at Aubrey as she sucked him and flicked herself, igniting every pleasure nerve in his body. Justin fought the nut back; he refused to bust all over the place before feeling Aubrey's walls.

As he enjoyed the slurping and sucking, Aubrey reached inside her bra and pulled out a Magnum condom. She administered protection with her mouth. By now, Justin's love rod was so hard that his tip throbbed and thumped. When Aubrey brought herself to orgasm, Justin almost let go. Her sweet, sexy moans turned him on so much. He moved her head away from his pelvis, picked her up, and faced her toward the mirror.

"Oh, so that's how you like it, daddy?" Aubrey moaned.

Justin was being mind-fucked and he loved it. Aubrey held on to the marble sink while staring at Justin in the mirror with her piercing grey eyes. Their eyes met as Justin slid his oversized, brick-hard love muscle deep inside Aubrey's cave. Aubrey let out a low whiney moan; she had not expected Justin to feel so good. With their eyes fixated on each other, Justin stroked her steady and deep. Their moans turned into loud lovemaking noises. They were enjoying each other so much that they forgot about Lynn in the dining room. Aubrey threw it back with each stroke. She came about two times, and Justin was still going strong trying to savor the moment. Aubrey's body began to move differently, gyrating uncontrollably. She was on the brink of an orgasm of orgasms. Justin could feel her walls tightening and pulling him in more with each stroke, and he knew he was not going to make it much longer. Aubrey scratched and grabbed for the walls as her hands slid down.

"Ohhh my God! I...I...I can't take it. Oooooh, this is...it. What's happening? OHHHHHHHHHHHH!" Aubrey yelled to the top of her lungs as she squirted everywhere.

Her once black lace was now white, and Justin's pelvis dripped of the creamy white substance. Justin blasted off right after that, quickening his strokes while holding both cheeks in his hands. Aubrey could not speak. She had never squirted like that before.

Just as Justin's eyes opened, he met Lynn standing in the doorway of the bathroom with papers in hand. He quickly reached for his trousers that were crumpled up at his feet. Aubrey could not move.

* * * * *

Brooke arrived home exhausted from her long day. She dropped her bag at the front door and proceeded toward the kitchen. She needed a double chocolate fix after her day. She had fumbled through her interview with Amber and almost got caught with Brenson. She poured her a large glass of Pinot Grigio as she let her ice cream unthaw on the counter. She flashed back to her encounter with Aubrey.

"That girl is nothing but trouble. If she thinks I'm calling her, she's crazy!" she said out loud.

Aubrey and Brooke knew each other from Atlanta when Brooke was in college. Brooke was a dancer under Jerome for a little less than a year, working to get some extra cash while in school. Aubrey had been her roommate freshman year. Brooke remembered that Aubrey was smart, but she had a sense of entitlement and an evil streak that was nothing short of treacherous. Aubrey forced a professor at the college into an affair, and when he would not do what she wanted him to do, she screamed rape and exposed their sex pictures to the university and his wife. Aubrey was so good at making up stories that she would almost believe them herself. Aubrey got Brooke involved in dancing under the false pretense that it was just dancing with bikinis on. Brooke was welcomed in at her audition. Her first performance was terrifying. Between sets, Jerome cornered her and threatened her with bodily harm if she did not get naked. A naive Brooke was scared and hundreds of miles away from home. The one friend she had betrayed her and ushered her into the lion's den. Jerome gave her some speech about having to complete her six-month contract or she would be hurt. Seeing Aubrey brought back terrible memories that no one but her and Aubrey shared. Brooke finally got away from the stripping scene when Aubrey dropped out of school after the scandal with the professor and began to strip full-time. Unfortunately, she did not escape before her and Aubrey's unforgettable encounter...

As usual, Brooke entered the club early to gather up her nerve to perform in front of all the losers that frequented the club. Upon her entering, she noticed the club was not as full like it normally was, and Jerome was sitting amongst the handful of men that was present. The stage was prepped, and Aubrey sat center stage. Brooke's first instinct was to run back out the door, but it was too late. Jerome approached her and gave her instructions.

"Hello, BB. You need to go get ready. Make it less than ten minutes. These good gentlemen here paid me nicely to shut the club down for a private show, and they want you and Bre to be the features."

"Jerome, I ain't with this shit. Why didn't you tell me this before--"

Jerome grabbed her arm forcefully. "Bitch, listen, I don't have to tell you shit. You're working your regular shift, right? Then get your ass in the back and be here in ten minutes, or I will come get your ass! Do I make myself clear?"

Brooke snatched her arm away, knowing Jerome was not bluffing. "Yeah, I understand."

While Brooke prepared for the show, Aubrey entertained the men with a few lap dances.Brooke emerged from the back ready to do her routines that she had practiced.

At least it's less dick I'll have to rub on and sure money out here, she thought to herself.

Brooke took a deep breath and approached the stage. She took center stage and gave the DJ the cue for her music. The men in the audience gave Brooke more confidence with their Ooo's and Aww's. The music began to play, but it was not her usual music. Brooke played it off and began to move to the music. She could see Aubrey slithering her way toward the stage as if she had practiced this routine for hours. Brooke was confused as to why Aubrey was getting in on her routine. Little did she know, she was the routine. The more they howled, the more Aubrey performed.

When Aubrey made it to the stage, the DJ slowed down the flow. Marcus Houston's "Naked" blasted through the speakers. Aubrey crawled cat-like toward Brooke. The group of about ten men surrounded the stage so they could be up close and personal to see the show. Aubrey reached out, grabbed Brooke's foot, and began to rub her hand up her leg. Brooke instantly tensed up. She began to dance around Aubrey, almost looking as if she was running from her. Jerome stood up and gave Brooke a look that could kill. Trying to take the focus off of Brooke's resistance, Jerome got up on stage and grabbed both women close.

"Let's hear it for this sexy duo. Let them know y'all are here to see them."

The small group of men went wild, throwing money on the stage and howling.

"That's more like it...motivation."

As the crowd cheered and asked for more, Jerome pulled Brooke close to him and pricked her side with his pocket knife. Then he leaned over and whispered in her ear, "Bitch, if you screw this money up for me, I will gut you like a fucking fish. Now, I expect you to act like you enjoy working with your friend and follow her lead, or let's just say this is your final performance. Keep smiling before I end it early."

Brooke trembled with fear. Jerome exited the stage, pumping his left fist in the air as the crowd cheered. The DJ spun the music back from the top. Aubrey danced around Brooke as she moved methodically to the slow beat. Brooke forced her body to obey the rhythm of the music. Aubrey got behind her and rubbed her body up against hers. Next, she smacked and kissed her bare bottom. Before Brooke realized it, Aubrey had both of them completely naked and her head was planted between her legs. Each slurp made Brooke war with reality and the pleasure that she was feeling. The reality was that Brooke was straight, but enjoying head from Aubrey tremendously.

After that night, Brooke knew she could not remain in the ATL and ever have a normal life. So, she planned a getaway and put it in motion two weeks after that, never to look back at Atlanta again. She moved back up north and ended up at Temple University.

Brooke snapped out of her daydream and took a long sip of her wine. She hated thinking about that time in her life. She was not happy to see Aubrey and was not impressed with her new look and attempted proper talk. In Brooke's mind, Aubrey was and always would be trouble.

Chapter 8
Southern Lockup

Spice awoke to the sound of her roomie yelling through the locked steel door and pressing her face against the door's small window. Her head ached, and she had crashed from all the coke that she consumed weeks ago. Spice attempted to lift her head, while struggling to open her mouth and tell her loud cellie to shut the hell up.

"Yo, shut the fuck up, Metta. What the hell is wrong with you? I have a pounding headache."

Metta turned to Spice and snarled, "Who the hell do you think you're talking to? We're not homeys and we're damn sure not friends. I will fuck you up in this cell, chica! I can't take this shit. It's too close in here."

The cell in the city prison was close quarters. The walls were a blah beige color and could put one to sleep if you stared at them for too long. The steel bunks were the slab of torture to their body night after night. Still groggy from a long night of torture, Spice sat up to attempt to protect herself from her crazy Mexican cellie. Spice, never being a fighter, had to prepare just in case she had to defend herself. Worn out with red bags under her eyes, Spice looked up at Metta from the bottom bunk as she stared down at her.

"Step the hell back, Metta, before you get what you're looking for!" Spice got into character quickly to save face.

Metta stepped to the right and grabbed Spice by the collar, pulling her up from the bed. Spice struggled and pushed against Metta's chest.

"Bitch, get off of me!"

The cell door opened suddenly, and the guard yelled, "Cindy Dorsey, step forward."

Metta quickly released her grasp, and Spice was never so happy to see the rude manly-looking correctional officer that usually tried to make advances at her.

Spice stepped up to the doorway and extended her arms out in front of her. The officer proceeded to secure her wrists and instructed her to step forward closer. Officer Truman leaned in and began patting Spice down to check for contraband. A confused Spice wondered where she was going and why. In the county, they transferred inmates without warning to another holding facility. Spice noticed her feet were not shackled, which meant she was not going on an outside transport.

Stocky-built Officer Truman ran her hands up Spice's legs slowly and then turned her around to face the wall as she ran her two fingers around the rim of her orange pants. Spice's body stiffened at the thought of her touching her. Officer Truman grew agitated, becoming rough and forceful as she led

70

Spice through the jail block. Spice could feel the tension in her tug, and therefore, was apprehensive to ask where she was going.

The pair walked through the long corridor past the master control satellite station that led them to the elevators. When they reached the last checkpoint, Officer Truman looked up at the camera as she waited for the officer in the bubble to buzz the door.

Spice took her chance to ask, "Truman, where are you taking me."

Clearly annoyed, Officer Truman responded, "You have an official visitor. Any more questions, Sherlock Holmes?"

Not wanting to seem as if she was challenging the officer, Spice looked down at the floor and said, "No, that's all."

Spice remembered the officer's brutal treatment to others that challenged her, and she recognized her potential to do her bodily harm if she wanted to.

The last checkpoint was cleared, and the two loaded the elevator. After the doors to the elevator closed, Officer Truman grabbed Spice's wrist shackles and pulled her close as she talked to her in a low, but stern tone.

"Who do you think you are, trick? You act as if you're better than somebody in this place. Your white ass came from the slums like the rest of them. Shaking your ass for money, but don't want to be touched by me. Bitch, please!"

Spice's heart raced; she was not happy to be on her bad side. "It's not like tha--"

The doors opened before Spice could finish, and Officer Truman escorted her past officers in the waiting area to a private room with a large window in the center of the wall. Inside sat a young, handsome African American man dressed in a well-pressed grey suit and bold red power tie, looking through what looked like a file. Spice entered first, and Officer

Truman followed. She pushed Spice down by her shoulders, sitting her in a silver metal chair facing the man in the suit.

Officer Truman caught eyes with the gentleman and said, "I will be right outside if you need me, sir.

He nodded and replied, "Okay, officer."

Spice watched the officer exit and breathed a sigh of relief.

"Hello, Cindy. I will be your lawyer for your trial. My name is William Sutton, and I am most happy to help you out of this shit storm that you are in."

Spice sat back in her chair as she watched William shuffle through papers. It was complete silence, and then...

"I'm fucking screwed. You look about nineteen years old, and you're a public defender. I'm going down! Oh shit, I'm really going up state for life," Spice cried hysterically.

William looked through his designer briefcase for a tissue. "Please don't cry, Ms. Dorsey. I can really help you, if you follow my advice."

He reached across the table and placed the tissue in her palm. Still crying, Spice wiped her tears and spoke in a high-pitched tone in between sniffles.

"You ain't no lawyer. How old are you? You look more like a model. Look at your damn briefcase and manicured nails. I'm screwed!"

Spice went on for about a few more minutes, while William continued shuffling through his notes.

"Look, Ms. Dorsey," he finally said, interrupting her ranting, "we only have forty-five minutes for this meeting, and you're wasting valuable time with the insults and crying. Get your shit together quickly or you will be up state for life!"

That got Spice's attention, and she started to listen intensely.

"From what my notes say and looking at the crime scene pictures, this is not looking good. You're being charged with murder one and felony possession of a controlled substance.

The drug charge is bogus, so I believe I can get you off of that one. However, the murder charges stick, and they are out for blood."

Spice sat there still listening with full attention.

"I recommend you take a plea down to manslaughter, a crime of passion."

Spice stood up, leaned in, and yelled, "Are fucking kidding me, you Cracker Jack lawyer! How 'bout murder none? I did not murder anyone. I loved Jerome and was devastated when I found him and Quanda dead, you prick. This is what you call a defense? Plea? Never, never never!"

Officer Truman entered the room when she heard the loud commotion. "Ms. Dorsey, sit and stay in your seat, or you will be removed!"

Spice sat back down in the chair as she attempted to control her wrath. Officer Truman exited the room and gave them the signal for twenty minutes.

"Listen, Ms. Dorsey, I know this may sound harsh, but the evidence they have against you is substantial, even without a weapon. With your belongings scattered about the scene, your heel being broken, which suggests you were running from the scene, you failing to contact the police, and finally your admitted relationship with Jerome, it would be hard to prove you're innocent."

Spice listened to her own lawyer sealing her fate. She lost it.

"Whose fucking lawyer are you?" Spice stood up again, this time not caring about the penalty. "One more time, I did not murder anyone! I found them both dead, and I ran! I ran! My Jerome..." She tossed her chair, while yelling to the top of her lungs. "No! No! He's gone, and you fucking want to make me suffer even more."

Crouched in the corner of the room, William yelled back, "I'm trying to help you, Ms. Dorsey, no matter how it seems."

Officer Truman rushed Spice and placed her in a restrictive hold. Spice was slammed to the floor and restrained. Her tears stained the cement floor as the officer pressed her face against the floor firmly.

"On your feet, Dorsey!" Officer Truman barked once Spice stopped struggling.

With her spirit broken and body hurting, she followed orders and staggered out of the meeting room. Still staying clear of her, William yelled her name as he held his briefcase under his right arm. Officer Truman reluctantly turned her to face William.

"You said two dead bodies, but it was only one. The female victim is alive barely, still in a coma with suspected massive brain damage."

Spice began sobbing uncontrollably. The small beacon of hope she had came and left that quickly. The only person that could clear her name was almost a vegetable with little hope of recovery.

Chapter 9
Nutcase Chase

Aubrey awoke to a knock on her front door. She rolled over to see the time. She was not expecting anyone and especially early in the morning. The clock next to her bed read 6:45 a.m. She decided to drift back to sleep, until she heard the same knocking again.

"Who the hell is at my door this damn early?"

Aubrey hurried to the door, not bothering to put on her robe. She swung the door open abruptly.

"How may I help you?!"

There stood Justin, peeking through three dozen of long-stemmed roses. "Good morning, sexy. This is an official wake up call."

Aubrey stepped to the side, still half asleep but happy to see him. Justin led a train of servants inside with polished silver dishes filled with a full-course breakfast, morning paper, and mail from the front desk. She showed them where to place everything, and Justin made himself comfortable.

An excited Aubrey winked at Justin, and in her country drawl said, "Thanks, babe. I'll be right with you. I need some water to touch this body."

Justin smiled. "You look as beautiful, as usual. Don't be too long."

Aubrey continued to the bathroom and turned the shower on to let the water temperature get just right while she brushed her teeth and put her face cleanser on. In the bedroom, Justin could hear the water running and got excited just thinking about her naked body under the streaming hot water. He nestled in the bed and turned the television on to catch the morning news.

"Hurry up, Aubrey. Don't want your food to get cold!" he yelled.

Aubrey answered him, but he couldn't make out her response due to the loud shower.

As the water poured down on her, she thought about her day and how full it would be. She had to order items for her new home, finalize papers, and be ready to receive delivery of her new Aston Martin Lagonda super-luxury SUV. Aubrey was so engrossed in her thoughts that she did not hear Justin enter the bathroom. A swift gust of air blew on the nape of her neck, followed by the sound of the shower closing and a warm kiss on the right side of her neck. She shivered at his touch, and her nipples became engorged from excitement. Aubrey remembered how good their last encounter had been. This would be their first real encounter fully disrobed and focused.

Justin ran his right hand down her smooth side as his manhood rested on her back. Aubrey let out a slow, low moan.

Justin had experienced her body once before and was very intrigued to experience her some more. Aubrey stretched both hands out and rested her breasts and torso against the marble shower wall. Justin started at the nape of her neck and licked straight down to her bare bottom, where he then softly kissed each cheek. Aubrey turned to face him and kissed his soft, full lips with just enough pressure. She moaned as their tongues danced like synchronized swimmers. Her moans brought him to full glory. He gently grabbed and fondled her supple breasts. At her height of desire, Aubrey wanted more contact. So, she jumped up and wrapped her legs around his waist as his hot rod penetrated her soft walls, meeting them like butter. Justin supported Aubrey's bottom with his forearms as she rode his stick like a jockey. He moaned with her as their pleasure intensified. Then Justin's arms began to shake.

"Oh, Aubrey, oh...this feels so good."

Aubrey knew Justin was a little more conservative than the guys she usually jumped in the sack with. She knew she had to turn up the freak if she was to have him where she wanted.

She let go of Justin's neck and contorted her body backward, placing one hand down at a time. She held her body up with both arms, while Justin was still inside of her. Aubrey then gyrated her hips in a circular motion as Justin's love stick hit every inch of her cave. Justin, now in a good groove, had his arms stretched as he palmed each side of Aubrey's hips.

"Damn, girl, this is some good lovin'."

Aubrey stopped moving.

Trying to keep the ultimate pleasure going while attempting to catch his breath, Justin asked, "What's going on baby? Don't stop."

Teasing him, Aubrey moved, then stopped, then moved and stopped again. "I need you to talk dirty to me to keep this pussycat purring."

Justin wanted more than anything to keep the session going. He had to think fast. Aubrey moaned, intensifying the moment.

"I want this tight, wet cunt all over me."

Aubrey, who was still upside down, cheered him on as she started to move slowly.

Justin grunted, "Errr, this is good."

"I need dirtier!" Aubrey ordered Justin to give her more grit if he wanted to continue.

Justin let out a loud roar as he gave her quick, hard thrusts. "This pussy is so wet. Mmm....ride this hard cock. Control this beast, bitch."

Aubrey could feel the tickle on her G-spot and could not tease him any longer. The faster Justin pumped, the louder they both became. With the combination of the blood rushing to Aubrey's head and the deep penetration, she could not hold back the climax. Justin was right in sync with her flow.

His forearms and biceps tightened, and he yelled, "Oh shit! I'm about to let off, baby!"

Aubrey yelled like a soprano, "Here I cum! Damn...here I cum!"

Her legs tightened around his waist, and they both squirted all over the place. Drained, they collapsed to the shower floor while attempting to catch their breath. Justin stared at Aubrey in amazement. After a couple minutes, Aubrey kissed him on the lips and stood to her feet to continue her shower.

Aubrey entered the bedroom with her towel wrapped around her beautiful frame. She opened the silver dish, took a piece of bacon, and bit it as she walked through the room. The clock read 7:30 a.m., and she was still tired, especially after her session with Justin. She turned the television up to watch the news. By this time, Justin was entering the bedroom, dancing like he belonged on the Chippendale lineup. Aubrey giggled and gestured for him to bring the food trays into bed with her. Justin crawled into bed next to Aubrey, and they began to enjoy the large spread he had ordered.

Justin leaned over and kissed her cheek. "That was amazing, Aubrey Green."

Aubrey smiled in response as she attempted to listen to the news for the weather. She had to know what to wear. A feed at the bottom of the screen said there was breaking news to report, and then the station cut to a newscaster standing in front of a scene that was blocked off with yellow caution tape.

"Violence and women in major cities are becoming more synonymous as the year marches on," the news anchor began. "This is the sixth violent crime in Atlanta involving murder at the hands of a woman. Weeks ago, two bodies were found in the home of this quiet tree-lined street, and it appears to have been a crime of passion. The house of strip club owner Jerome Kobbs, also known as Rome, was turned into a torture chamber, and this woman..." The station flashed a picture of the accused on the screen. "...Cindy Dorsey has been charged with first-degree murder. If convicted, she could face life in prison. Why are our women turning to gruesome violence? How can this trend be broken? Stay tuned for the story at eleven."

Aubrey sat there with her mouth open as she thought, How did Spice get clipped for this, and what does she really know about that night? I'll have to pay her a visit and find out.

Justin had been talking to Aubrey, but with her so deep in thought, he only sounded like background noise.

"Aubrey, are you alright? You seem like you're in a trance."

She snapped out of it. "What? Oh, I just can't believe the violence in this world."

Justin stared at her and continued. "I asked if you know her. She's from your town."

Aubrey became defensive. "Why the hell do I have to know ole girl just because we're from the same city? Look, Justin, I had fun, but I have to organize my day, and I need to be focused to do so. I'll call you later."

"Oh, so now I'm getting put out after that great session. Love 'em and leave 'em, huh?"

Aubrey was so preoccupied with her thoughts that she did not even respond to Justin. By the time she finally looked up, he was dressed and headed to the door.

"Thanks for everything, Justin. I'll see you later."

"Yes, I better see you. We have a date at the Kimmel Center."

Aubrey continued to eat her breakfast as she did some writing. She usually wrote to get rid of anxiety and when she was upset. As she tapped her pen on her pad, she paused to gather her next thought. Aubrey was getting anxious because she had not heard back from any publishers she had reached out to. She wanted to at least get a meeting with their submissions department before she continued submitting new work.

Aubrey did send her script to one local publishing house, Legendary Reads Publishing Group or LRP. They were one of the top publishing houses in Philly and had a bomb pen squad. Aubrey did her research on the owner of the company and felt LRP was where she wanted to grow her career. Brea Tillman was thirty-five years old and a very successful publisher of African American fiction. She had a grassroots story that appealed to Aubrey. The fact that she was said to read every manuscript before it was approved or denied and met with her authors regularly for feedback on upcoming projects stood out. Always looking to fit in somewhere, Aubrey romanticized the experience of getting an acceptance letter from LRP for her script, Southern Sassy. She felt they could be the family that she always wanted, and she could finally be accepted for more than what was between her legs. Aubrey had a new location, new number, and new career path.

Aubrey continued to map out her day, and she browsed her to-do list. She had already called the car dealership and was expecting her custom Aston Martin in the matter of an hour. It was only 9:30 a.m., but already she had completed several tasks. Aubrey scanned the channels for some good daytime television and then checked on the delivery of her furniture. Her closing day was approaching in a few days, and she would be saying goodbye to her penthouse. Aubrey moved her papers around on the bed and looked through the mail.

"Oh my God, it came!" she shouted.

In her hand was a letter from LRP. She was nervous to open it, but excited at the same time. Writing had always been personal to her. That was why she did not share her writing with anyone since her mother shot her down in her youth. Aubrey's hands shook at the thought of opening it. She felt nauseous as she carefully used the letter opener along the edge. She unfolded the letter as she talked to herself, assuring herself that she deserved for her dreams to come true. Aubrey *fixated her eyes on the letter as she read.*

Dear Ms. Green,

We received your submission to our office and have reviewed the first five chapters. In an effort to expand our readership, we are seeking stories that are set in various locations with characters that are developed well beyond the east coast. We would like to further discuss your manuscript Southern Sassy in our office. Please contact us to schedule a time and date that is convenient for you. Please bring two copies of the entire manuscript at the time of the meeting. Call our office at the number provided below.

Sincerely,
Renee Rice
Vice President of the Submissions Department

Aubrey was excited that they wanted to meet with her. She could finally move on with her life and experience the next chapter. Aubrey called the company immediately.

"Thanks for calling LRP. How may I help you?"

"Hello, my name is Aubrey Green, and I received a letter instructing me to call for an appointment."

"Okay, ma'am, what color was your letter?"

Aubrey paused and then said, "Color?"

"Yes, the color of the paper the letter was printed on."

"Oh, it was on green paper."

"Okay. That means you are a priority submission. Can you come in this afternoon about three o'clock?"

Aubrey did not want to seem desperate. So, she told the woman, "Hold, please. Let me check my schedule."

"Okay, I will hold."

After a few seconds, Aubrey told her, "This afternoon seems to be clear. Can you please give me directions? I will be driving, but I'm new to the area."

"Sure. Give me your email address, and I will send you all of the information you need to know."

After providing her information, Aubrey ended the call. She was a little annoyed that Brea Tillman's name was not on the letter, and she started to wonder if she had even seen the script.

Aubrey headed to her closet to put together the perfect power outfit. She had a deal to land, and she wanted to look good doing it.

She walked into the massive closet and took a gander at all of the clothes that she had accumulated over the past three weeks. Her closet was anything but neat. She had been tearing through it putting together her various "going out" threads, not to mention attempting to pack for her upcoming move.

Aubrey attempted to make sense of the mess. She sifted through her blazers, then skirts, and finally shirts. She took about thirty minutes to find what she thought to be the perfect outfit. Pleased with her selection, Aubrey clawed her way from the floor of the closet and headed for the bedroom. She smiled as she prepared herself for her beauty ritual.

Aubrey pulled her long, black hair up in a sloppy bun. Still in her undergarments, she danced across the floor, happy to be getting ready for a meeting of a lifetime. Then a feeling of sadness overcame her as she thought about her mother and not being able to share this special moment with her.

"Shit, Mom!" Aubrey yelled. "Even in my good moments, you creep in and fuck them up. I will be somebody besides a man's whore. I hope you get to see that day wherever you are!"

Aubrey hated thinking about her mother and hated even more the feelings associated with the thought. Pushing those thoughts out of her mind, she continued to get dressed.

* * * * *

Justin started his workday checking on major accounts in the hotel and making sure his line staff was on point. He called the Chart House Seafood restaurant to make reservations for his and Aubrey's outing. As he hung up the phone, a tall, white gentleman approached the desk and asked for the manager.

"Hello, how may I help you?" Justin asked, interrupting the gentleman and the front desk clerk.

"Hi. My name is Mat from Mainline Porsche, and I have a delivery for one of your guests."

"I can help you with that. I'm Justin, the hotel manager. What's the guest's name?"

The delivery man looked through his papers. "Aubrey Green."

Justin looked through the glass of the front door and saw a pearl white Aston Martin with cranberry red leather interior. There was also a Porsche SUV double parked with a man dressed in a blue suit sitting in the driver's seat.

"Okay. I will contact her now. Please have a seat in our lounge area. I will alert you when she arrives."

Justin contacted Aubrey to alert her that she needed to sign for her car. When Aubrey did not answer, he left a message that he flagged as urgent. He managed to remain professional despite the personal nature of him and Aubrey's relationship. He was curious as to what Aubrey did and how she had so much money to spare. Seeing the showroom Aston Martin parked outside the hotel was the first time Justin questioned if he could keep up with her.

Twenty minutes after Justin left the message, Aubrey emerged from the elevator looking stunning. She adorned her feet with black wedge booties. Traveling up her legs was her signature designer stockings. Her outfit was put together well. She wore a heather- gray tailored pencil skirt and a turquoise satin blouse with the high bow-neck neatly tucked in her belted waist. Aubrey's tailored jacket fell perfectly at her waist as a subtle ruffled tail framed the back. She splashed her ensemble with a butter-soft, red, oversized clutch that she used as a briefcase. Justin's mouth was stuck open. He knew she was beautiful, but her hair pulled up in a bun confirmed it; she was flawless.

As Aubrey approached the front desk, Justin waved for Mat to come meet her. Mat was already following her with his eyes and loins. He also approached the desk. Justin cleared his throat to break Mat out of his trance.

"Mat, this is Ms. Aubrey Green."

Mat was happy to show Aubrey to her new ride. As Aubrey took the keys and began to follow Mat, Justin could not control the urge to let him know she was taken.

He quickly blurted out, "See you tonight, babe."

Aubrey chuckled and said, "See then, Justin."

Justin felt silly as Aubrey and Mat made their way outside.

Chapter 10
Scottie's World

The day was off to a great start. Scottie was halfway through his to-do list, and it was only a little past eleven o'clock. He sat at his oversized slate desk taking in the chic atmosphere. Scottie appreciated his success like nobody understood. From the time when he was a young man, he had a plan that he stuck to. Coming from an upper middleclass family, he knew how the finer side of life looked. His father made sure of that. Scottie's determination to be successful was fueled by two things: his love for good living and his hatred toward his father. Scottie strived hard to remain on top so he would never need to ask his father for anything. He possessed a hatred for him ever since that day from years ago when he found out about his brother. Scottie had always looked up to his father and could not believe he stepped out on his mother, let alone had a child that he did not take care of.

Scottie's office was located on the second floor in the center of the club, with his desk positioned directly in front of an eight-foot stenciled glass wall. The imported marble floors had hues of silver and deep black. Accents of polished nickel were throughout, and fine black art hung on the wall. To the left of his desk was a lounge area that was functional for entertaining after-hour company or conducting a business meeting with potential clients.

Club Intoxic was sure to be another hit. Only days away from the big launch party, Scottie was quite pleased with himself. He had a great team to thank for that, which included his brother and his close friend Brooke.

Scottie drifted off in deep thought. He was unsure why Brooke had been acting so strangely at their meeting and was concerned the pressure from the grand opening was getting to her. He decided to give Brooke a call to ask her to meet up with him later.

"Hello. Sorry I missed your call, but our connection is important to me. So, leave a detailed message at the end of the beep."

Scottie followed the directions on Brooke's answering machine.

"Hello, Brooke. This is your boss. I need you to meet me at Creshiem Cottage Café at twelve-thirty. I have something we need to discuss. See you soon."

He looked at the clock positioned on his transparent bookcase. Scottie had a standing twelve o'clock lunch meeting at the café once a week. So, he figured he would kill two birds with one stone.

* * * * *

Across town, Brooke was in her office at the cooperate headquarters located above Scottie's club, Shot Runner. Shot Runner was the first club Scottie opened, and he attributed his success to his beginning. Scottie started out leasing the place, and within a couple of years, the success of his second club afforded him the opportunity to purchase the building. He felt the main office should always be housed there, like a sense of home where it all began.

Brooke wrestled with her bag to reach her ringing telephone. Brenson stroked her inner thigh, making her grasp on the strap inadequately. He was south of the boarder, trying to enjoy a mid-morning snack, and did not want to let go.

"Let it ring, Brookie," he affectionately urged her.

"Oh...Bren, wait a minute. That could have been Scottie."

Brenson made full contact as he kissed her wet spot, going in for the kill.

"So what. Let him wait. Some things are more important than his wants and needs," Brenson said softly in between slurps.

Brooke's body was at war with her mind. She was holed up in her office mid-morning with the door locked and in a compromising position. Her behavior was wrong on so many levels. Brenson's soft, wet tongue glided over her perky, hard clitoris just right. In bliss, she arched her back.

"Emmm, Bren...emmmmm, we're on the cloooock."

Brenson's oral skills provoked sexiness in every word Brooke uttered. Brenson loved Brooke's body and could not get enough of her goodies. His insatiable appetite for her was also fueled by his envy of Scottie. Knowing he had something that Scottie wanted increased Brenson's interest.

"And you're being paid handsomely."

As he said the last word in his sentence, he knew that he had Brooke where he wanted her. She let out a loud, sexy moan as her juices flowed down Brenson's chin and onto her cherry wood desk.

The fun was over, and Brooke awkwardly slid off of her desk. Brenson stood in the center of the floor still rubbing his rod, while staring at Brooke. His adrenaline was on overdrive, and he loved the idea of ravishing Brooke in her office. He knew their naughtiness would burn Scottie up.

Brooke wobbled to the left as she made her way to the private bathroom in the corner of the spacious office. She had to clean up and get the air fresher. The air was infused with hot sex, and she could not risk someone else being exposed to her and Brenson's love essence. She looked in the mirror and stopped in her tracks when she saw the person staring back at her. The behavior she was displaying was not her norm.

"What the hell am I doing?" she whispered.

Brooke knew hot sex was great in its place, but her and Brenson were going nowhere fast, and on top of that, she had to keep their escapades a secret. A tap at the door brought Brooke out of her daydream. Brenson entered the bathroom to a naked-from-the-waist-down Brooke staring in the mirror.

"Hey, babe, what's up? Are you cool? Do you have room at that sink so I can freshen up, too?"

With a fake smile, Brooke looked at Brenson through the reflection in the mirror. "Everything's fine. I'm just admiring how good sex looks on me. And, yes, it's always room at my sink for you."

Brenson smiled, and Brooke slid to her right to continue to freshen up her personals.

Both Brenson and Brooke refreshed, and after putting themselves back together, they embraced and shared a kiss. As Brenson exited Brooke's office, she gestured for him to close her door. Brooke then nestled in her desk chair and began reviewing her long to-do list.

While planning out the remainder of her day, she dialed her voicemail. Brooke's eyes grew wide as Scottie's words played in her ear. She glanced at the clock on her side table. The time read 12:18 p.m. Brooke had less than fifteen minutes to make it across town to meet Scottie. She almost toppled over in her five-inch heels as she scrambled to gather all of her belongings and head out the door. She knew Scottie hated for anyone to be late, and she was worried about what he wanted to discuss. Brooke's mind raced and her anxiety was extremely high. She could not imagine Scottie wanting to talk about anything good.

The gridlocked twelve o'clock traffic stretched for about three blocks. Brooke could not keep it together. Deciding to let Scottie know she was running late, she reached in her bag to retrieve her phone. She hit the speed dial button for his number, and the phone began to ring. However, all three times she tried to reach him, she was greeted by his voicemail.

"Shit!" she yelled. Frustrated with so many things, that's all she could get out.

Finally, traffic began to move, and she was on her way.

* * * * *

Scottie sat on the wooden bench in the waiting area. The small upscale cottage was the ideal place for lunch. With its interior styled like a cozy home, the cottage had several different rooms for private dining. The hostess was very in tuned with their regulars, Scottie being one of them. She approached the waitress and instructed her where to seat him once his guest arrived.

The door of the cottage opened, and Scottie's face lit up. In strutted a stylish older woman who had everyone in the area looking at her well-put-together outfit. Scottie stood up and greeted her with a hug.

"Hello, Mom. You're looking good, as usual."

As Scottie took her by the hand, Mrs. Boyd stepped back in a playful manner and gave him a spin.

"I feel just fine, too, son. Where do you think you get your looks from?"

They both shared a laugh.

The waitress stood to the side as not to interrupt their greeting. After the laughter stopped, she politely said, "Right this way, sir."

Scottie and Mrs. Boyd followed her to their private dining area. The waitress took Mrs. Boyd's coat and placed it on the coat rack in the center of the room. The small room had a marble table that sat four. The windows in the room served as the frame for their beautiful backdrop. Outside, pretty white snow still framed the sidewalks and cobblestone streets. They could see the cars go to and fro up and down Germantown Avenue.

The waitress allowed the two to get comfortable as she lit the wood-burning fireplace. Scottie thanked her and drink orders were placed. As the waitress turned to leave the room, Scottie gently touched her left arm.

"Excuse me, Amanda. There will be another guest joining us. Please bring a place setting for her and a menu, as well."

Mrs. Boyd gave Scottie a look of confusion. She knew he never brought girls to meet her; he had a rule about that. She waited until Amanda walked away before she grilled Scottie about the mystery guest.

"Scottie who is joining us? Where is she from...?"

Scottie laughed, and with a half grin, he responded, "Mom, please. You know you're the only girl in my life. Brooke is meeting us. I feel she's working too hard and needs an intervention."

Mrs. Boyd smiled. "Oh, my Brookie will be here? How nice. I miss seeing her like before."

Scottie knew where the conversation was going. He took a deep breath. "Like before when, Mom?"

Mrs. Boyd gave Scottie a look that could kill. Their playful lunch turned serious quickly.

"Don't take that tone with me, Scotdale Jr. Like before you moved out years ago after college and never visit the house anymore...how you never visit your father. When are you going to forgive him? I have. I know you were hurt about the whole Brenson thing, but you got a brother who adores you out of the deal. Scottie, people make mistakes, you know, but we must forgive."

Scottie hated to have the conversation about his dad. "Mom, I can't tell you how or when to forgive, and you cannot do that to me, either. Dad gave me Brenson, which is true, but at what cost? I do not want to discuss it anymore!"

Mrs. Boyd knew she could pull rank if she wanted to, but she decided against it and left it alone. She did not want to ruin the time she had with her Scottie.

"Okay, Jr., you win. So what's new?"

The waitress returned with their drinks that would help to lighten the mood.

Pulling his drink closer to him, Scottie said, "Thanks, Amanda."

* * * * *

Brooke finally arrived and could see the small cottage sitting on the corner of the block. She pulled up and made a left inside the parking lot. Then she hurried out of her truck to make the light to cross the street. Struggling, she reached in her oversized Louis Vuitton bag to grab her gloves. Her hands were freezing. Brooke's heels on her boots got stuck in the grooves of the cobblestone street, and she almost fell to the ground as she tripped over the trolley tracks.

"Damn it! This street is screwed up. Charm my ass!" Brooke yelled.

A gentleman in a white-on-white Benz gave her a wink as he rode by. Brooke, who was late and unsure of what she was walking into, waved him off as she tipped along on her toes like a ballerina. She stumbled in the door, hair beat from the wind and frustrated. The hostess gave a double take. Brooke knew she must have looked tore up.

"Hello, I am here to meet Mr. Boyd."

The hostess waved the waitress down. Amanda led the way, saying, "Follow me, ma'am." Brooke obliged her, but hated to be called ma'am. She smoothed her hair down with her hand, while looking at her watch and taking a deep breath. She was twenty minutes late and feeling uneasy about the meeting.

* * * * *

Brenson sat in his office crunching numbers for the many business ventures Scottie was involved in. Good at what he did, Brenson kept Scottie's empire running smoothly with no wrinkles in the fabric. Brenson also stole enough off the top of each project to buy a small town. He always justified his "extras" as necessary due to the life he lived growing up on the wrong side of the tracks, while Scottie had what he always wanted: a father with stability and money.

As he cleaned up the books and made sure all was together, he thought about how long it would be before he could break away from Scottie and take everything he loved. He thought about Brooke and the amazing sex they had. He liked Brooke, but knew he did not love her. Brenson had to have her, though. Taking Scottie's money was not enough; he had to win the ultimate prize: Brooke's hand in marriage. Brenson knew in order to really make his plan sting like he had planned that he would need to have the timing down to a science. Getting Brooke to fall in love with him had become his top priority. Making her squirt was effortless, so he felt connecting that to emotions would not be hard.

* * * * *

Scottie stood up when Brooke entered the room. He leaned over and gave her a kiss on the cheek. Brooke was glowing. Scottie could see her beauty even through her disheveled appearance.

"Hey, Mrs. Boyd," Brooke said with excitement as she reached over to give her a big hug.

"Hello, Brookie. I've missed you."

As the two women continued to embrace, Scottie cleared his throat as if to remind them that he was still there.

"I give your tore up behind a kiss...but all I get is a hello. See, Mom? That's why I'm still single!"

Brooke replied, "No, you're single because nobody can deal with your picky ass for more than thirty days."

They all laughed. Brooke breathed a sigh of relief; she was in the clear as long as Mrs. Boyd was in the mix.

Scottie raised his glass. "To my two favorite girls. A man shouldn't be so lucky to have a wonderful mother and a beautiful business partner and friend...Salute!"

They all clinked their glass as both women replied, "Salute!"

Chapter 11
Chance Meeting

Aubrey followed the directions of her GPS as if her life depended on it. She could not wait to get to her meeting and hear the million-dollar deal that she would be offered. The wheels on Aubrey's new ride rotated with such precision that she felt as if she was floating on air. The power under the hood was unreal. One tap of the gas pedal and she was gone.

Aubrey made a right onto the expressway as instructed by the GPS. She was about two exits away from her destination. Aubrey was ecstatic, but had no one with whom she could share her excitement. She had just met Justin and was not that deep into him. She really needed a mother at that point. She needed a connection. Her grandmother was her rock, but she had not spoken with her since she left Atlanta. She wondered how she was doing, but would not risk calling to find out just in case they had her in rotation in relation to Jerome and Quanda's murder. She thought about what the news had reported and was not too sold that Spice would take the fall.

"How the hell did Spice get caught up?" Aubrey spoke aloud.

Her GPS brought her out of her daze. Exit 13 in one mile on your left, the computerized voice told her. She was finally going to move forward, but she could not shake the people in her past. After making a couple of turns off of the exit, Aubrey reached her destination. She pulled up in front of a tall building on the north side of downtown. Then she grabbed her red clutch, handed the valet attendant the valet key to her vehicle, and headed inside the building.

The lobby was busy with businessmen and businesswomen buzzing throughout. Behind the information desk that anchored the room sat a heavyset older women reading the newspaper. Aubrey walked up and cleared her throat, waiting to be acknowledged. The lady continued to read. The front of the paper had a headline that read Special Edition Philly Entrepreneurs in the Spotlight. Aubrey cleared her throat again. This time, the woman placed the newspaper down, while placing her finger in between the pages to save her spot. Aubrey looked at the front cover. The guy pictured looked familiar, but she brushed it off.

"May I help you?" the lady asked with an attitude.

Aubrey's eyes traveled from the paper to her face. In her most professional voice, she replied, "I am looking for the office of LRP. Do I need to sign in?"

The lobby attendant took a deep breath and exhaled. "Yes, you need to sign in, and I need to call them. Do you have your paperwork requesting the meeting with you?"

"Yes, I do. Just a minute," Aubrey replied, her eyes traveling back to the newspaper.

Realizing Aubrey was attempting to read upside down, the attendant told her, "You know you can have a free paper. They are to your left in the wire bin."

Aubrey turned, looked at the bin, and gave her a fake smile.

The attendant hung the phone up and pointed Aubrey in the direction of the elevators. "They are expecting you. Take the middle elevator and get off on the fifth floor."

"Thanks for the paper," Aubrey said, then headed toward the elevator while folding the paper and placing it in her purse.

She entered the elevator and sarcastically waved at the lobby attendant. As soon as the doors closed, she laughed until she realized she had not gotten the suite number. Her stomach churned as the power from the elevator ascending gave her flutters in her gut. The elevator stopped, and in a race with time, a worried Aubrey scanned the letter from LRP for the suite number. When the elevator doors opened, Aubrey's eyes lifted from the paper, and her body moved forward, obeying her legs. Aubrey's brain could not translate everything her eyes were taking in fast enough.

Aubrey had fallen into the lap of luxury. The office was immaculate. The white marble floors extended as far as the eye could see. Hues of turquoise, stark white, emerald green, and gold floated throughout the space. Wiped cherry wood inlays on the wall matched the office furniture. The office manager greeted Aubrey.

"Hello, Ms. Green. Do you have the items that were requested?"

While still scanning the place, Aubrey extended her arm, handing him the papers.

"I'll take those, and you can have a seat right over there in the waiting area."

Aubrey nodded and headed over to the white sofa with oversized pillows. Anxious about her meeting, she wanted to hear a familiar voice. She had laid low in Philly for a while and was trying to rationalize contacting her grandmother. Aubrey always called or went to her house when she was in trouble or needed reassurance. She hated how insecure she was, but had no knowledge of how to change it. She wondered how her grandmother would receive her since she had not spoken to her in over four weeks and had disconnected her other cell phone. Aubrey didn't even know if her grandmother would answer for an unknown number. Aubrey pulled her cell phone from her purse and dialed the number anyway.

As soon as the phone rang once, a tall lady dressed in a business suit called Aubrey for her meeting. She hit the end button, took a deep breath, and headed to her destiny.

* * * * *

Brooke was relieved the lunch she had with Scottie was not at all what she expected. Scottie was concerned about her being stressed out and offered to get her some extra help with the Bossin' Up Ball. Brooke smiled at the thought of the time spent with Scottie and Mrs. Boyd, most of all Scottie. Old feelings she thought had diminished resurfaced after hanging out with the Boyd's.

As she drove away from their meeting place, she began to feel tortured in her soul. Screwing Brenson several times a week was lovely for the complexion, but poison to her conscious. Aubrey headed for the only place she knew would heal her sorrow. Retail therapy was her favorite pick-me-up, and she planned to tear her favorite boutique out of the frame. Just as she planned to heal from moral suicide and gush over her time spent with Scottie, her phone vibrated against the bottom of her purse. Aubrey swerved as she tried to retrieve it.

"This better be important damnit." She found her electronic treasure. The traffic light turned red just in time. "Hello!" an agitated Brooke shouted into the phone.

"Hello, sexy," a masculine voice said smoothly.

Brooke knew who the voice belonged to.

"Hey, Bren. What's going on?"

"I was just thinking of you and wanted to see you later on...dinner, then you and dessert. How does that sound?"

Aubrey looked up at the sky and whispered, "Really? Right now, God?"

Brenson looked at the phone to be sure his volume was turned up. "What did you say, Brooke? I can't here you clearly."

Brook chuckled. "I wasn't talking to you. I'm out right now. I'll call you later."

Brenson was not feeling the change he heard in Brooke's voice. "Are you okay? What's wrong?"

Brooke tried to perk up. "Bren Bren, I'm fine. I'll call you later."

As Brooke ended the call, she knew she would have to end their affair sooner than later.

* * * * *

Aubrey thought she could not be more impressed until she entered the office for her meeting. The hand-carved door plaque read Renee Rice, Vice President. Renee's office looked like an apartment. A white plush rug sat in the center of the room and stretched out toward each wall. The marble floors peaked out from the sides of the rug. She had an executive oval table with six leather turquoise chairs to the left of her custom-made cherry wood desk and a matching turquoise sofa with emerald silk pillows. On her wall-to-wall bookshelf sat various awards and plaques for outstanding quality and hard work in the industry.

The receptionist, who was a different one than the front desk receptionist, asked Aubrey to have a seat at the table, and then the receptionist sat on the opposite side and booted up her laptop in preparation of the meeting. Renee entered the room alone and addressed Aubrey with a handshake.

"Hello, Ms. Green. I'm Renee Rice, VP here at LRP. I'm glad you could make it here today."

"Thanks for having me. I am excited to get started. I usually don't share my writing."

Renee looked through a white file while Aubrey spoke, not even making eye contact.

"Okay, let's get down to business. We liked your story. Well, we think it has potential. The life in Atlanta for this young girl "Sassy" is very interesting, from her upbringing to how she made her money. The good news is that your characters are three dimensional."

Aubrey sat back in her chair. Feeling herself getting angry, she tried to slow her breathing. "I'm glad you like the story so far. Thank you for the opportunity."

Aubrey gave Renee several times to alter her behavior and stop treating her like she was not there. Her mother used to do the same thing, and she hated it.

Renee continued. "I would like to go over the contract with you and discuss what we here at LRP are willing to offer you for the manuscript."

Aubrey removed her hands off of the table and placed them in her lap. The receptionist was taking notes, but could see Aubrey getting upset. Being a get-down-to-business no-nonsense person, Renee was missing a human element to her personality. Aubrey's left leg began to shake, and she dug her nails in her skin trying not to snap.

Aubrey interrupted Renee. "Ms. Rice, is Mrs. Tillman available? I would like to meet her. I read about how she is involved in all of the submissions that get called back."

Renee gave Aubrey a look as if to say, I don't have time for this groupie mess.

Renee cleared her throat. "Mrs. Tillman has a meeting at this time. She will join us after she's done. Now, if you don't mind, we really need to move on so we can get through the business and paperwork. Chaé here needs to type up what we agree on so you can take a copy with you to have your lawyer look over the paperwork within ten days."

Not liking Renee's tone or attitude, Aubrey dug in her leg a little harder, while Renee continued.

"We are prepared to give you a five-thousand-dollar advance and thirty percent royalty on all book sales less returns. Once you provide us with the new version of the story, you get another ten-thousand-dollar advance. We really believe in your story and know with some changes to the storyline and title we will see success."

Aubrey stood up at and looked Renee in the eyes. "Change the story...and name? I don't think so. I need to see Mrs. Tillman now. This is not at all what I expected. You can't even look me in the face. Do you have any idea how long it took me to write that story that you just speak about like it's a casual thing?"

Chaé, the receptionist, stopped typing and backed up from the table. She was not sure what was going to happen. No one had ever talked to Renee that way. LRP had an ironclad system. Renee was the pit-bull that was always sent in first to lay the groundwork, and then Mrs. Tillman would come in at the end to smooth the deal over after the author had signed the contract. Renee was a good read on people. She pictured Aubrey as being a tough sale, so she threw in a five percent extra royalty split in order to reel her in. Checking out

Aubrey's clothes and seeing the symbol on her car key let Renee know what she was driving and made her go for it.

Renee stood to her feet, as well. "Ms. Green, please have a seat. No one meant to offend you."

Continuing to stand, Aubrey told her, "Ms. Rice, no one didn't offend me. You did! Mrs. Tillman, please."

A swift wind tickled the back of Aubrey's neck. She turned and there stood a woman with smooth brown skin and shoulder-length hair cut into a bob. Aubrey recognized her from the many pictures on their website and in business magazines. She was as pretty in person as in the pictures. Dressed in an all-black tailored dress and red-bottom ankle boots, she extended a hand to Aubrey.

"Hello, Ms. Green. I am Mrs. Brea Tillman, owner of LRP. Please have a seat. I apologize for my lateness. I was on a business call, and it lasted longer than I expected."

Mrs. Tillman was definitely the "good cop". Her presence calmed the tension in the room.

"Renee, did you explain to Ms. Green how excited we are to extend a publishing deal to her for Southern Sassy?"

Renee attempted to control her emotions. "Yes. That is what we were discussing before you walked in."

Aubrey cleared her throat. "Actually, we were discussing how Ms. Rice wanted to change my masterpiece."

Renee gave Aubrey a look to calm down.

Brea Tillman continued. "Well, with any masterpiece, we always have to get it ready for the public. That's why editors exist in our world. Let me start by saying the characters are so real. You made us feel for them all...even the worthless mother. There are some things that need to be changed, but we can discuss that throughout the process."

Feeling a lot better, Aubrey sat back in the chair. Brea Tillman was okay after all. Seeing Aubrey more relaxed, Brea instructed Chaé to continue typing up the details of the contract as they discussed it. Then she continued to discuss the story.

"Ms. Green, the plot does need some changes to be more believable. For instance, Sassy's relationship with her mother seems a little unrealistic. She continues to accept the horrible treatment, and she is viewed too much as a victim. Sassy was very smart with her decision to use men in order to get her needs met, but her common sense failed her with her mother."

Aubrey stood up, and this time, she refused to sit. "What did you say? If you had any common sense, you would have actually read the five chapters of the damn book that I sent to you before coming to the meeting! You are a disgrace. Here I am admiring you for how you run your business, and you are a fucking fraud. All you want to do is rape first-time authors and wrap it up in a pretty bow. If the magazines could see you now, Ms. I Read All Submissions, Especially For the Ones That We Offer Contracts! You think you can disrespect me by not even meeting with me first, and then come in here trying to butter me up when things were going south with your trained pit-bull? Now you insult me, too. You can take your contract and shove it up your ass! Oh, and for your information, Mrs. Owner, Sassy killed the mother by chapter three!"

Brea was shocked at how Aubrey behaved.

It took her a minute, but before Aubrey could show herself out, Brea replied, "Contract won't be stuck up anybody's ass! You and this 'Cat in the Hat' first book...you should be grateful we even responded back to your ass. Your behavior demonstrates why you will never get published by anyone but yourself. Ms. Country Ghetto Star, every author has to change things in their manuscript. Who the hell do you think you are? Find your way out of my establishment before you get carried out!"

Aubrey lunged across the table, but Renee grabbed her by her arm. Chaé, who was knocked to the floor in the scuffle, managed to crawl to safety and call for security. Aubrey snatched away from Renee and gave Brea a look that could kill.

"For your information, bitches, I can give you both twenty thousand dollars. So, don't fucking insult me." With that, she picked up her clutch from the floor and then exited the office with furry in her boiling blood.

Aubrey swore the entire ride down to the lobby. Once she exited the elevator, she adjusted her clothes and headed to valet.

* * * * *

Brooke had a shopping outing that would cure anyone's blues. She found all of her favorite designers at Upper Flow Boutique. She packed her trunk with all of her goodies. Shoes, dresses, and a few pair of designer jeans occupied her frilly shopping bags. When she got into the car, she realized Brenson had called her again. She was thinking of taking him up on his offer.

Brooke started the car and proceeded to pull off. As she approached the third traffic light, she made a right turn and almost rode up on the curb. There stood Aubrey in front of the Tower Palace building fixing her hair and talking to herself. She was confused as to why Aubrey was dressed in business attire. In her rearview mirror, she saw the valet pull up in a pearl white Aston Martin. Brooke's eyes widened as big as fifty-cent pieces.

Aubrey Green, what are you up to? Brooke thought to herself.

Aubrey was furious. She had just been disrespected to the highest level in her eyes, and it was unacceptable.

"Who the hell did she think she was messing with?" Aubrey said out loud to herself. "Weak? How is murdering someone who wronged you being weak? Didn't even read my shit...the nerve of her. She called me down here to make a fool of me. That's why I don't share my writing. They don't understand me!"

The valet pulled up and saw Aubrey pacing and talking as if she had someone listening. Aubrey tipped the valet and took possession of her vehicle. As she made a right around the corner, she searched for a café to get a light snack. Spotting one, Aubrey double parked and hopped out to get a coffee and pastry. Aubrey's car got many looks as people passed by the stylish ride. Once Aubrey got her snack, she got back in the car and attempted to find a place to park. Seeing someone getting in their car to leave, Aubrey waited for the blue Buick to pull out and then she slid into the spot neatly. Aubrey unwrapped her pastry, took a sip of her coffee, and then pulled out the newspaper to kill some time. She unfolded the paper and began scanning the front page for the mystery man, but his picture was too small to really see him.

He's a nice looking guy. Maybe that's why I thought he was familiar, she thought to herself. Aubrey turned the page and then again until she found the article on the mystery man, listing him as one of the most successful self-made businessmen in Philadelphia.

The newspaper had a major spread on Scottie and his chief officers. Brooke's picture was amongst the photos with an extensive write up about the Bossin' Up Ball at Scottie's new club, Club Intoxic. Aubrey thought she was tripping. Her mouth hung open for about five minutes.

"This is the guy that I ran into when I first got here. Brooke knows him, and they're having a ball. I'm there and date-free, just in case."

Aubrey looked up at the dashboard. The time read 5:20 p.m.

"Shit, I'm supposed to meet Justin in less than a half hour," she said aloud.

The search for her cell phone began. After moving items around in her purse, she found her cell phone in the deep pocket on the purse's lining. Knowing Justin would be disappointed, she prepared herself to use her sexy, cute voice to soften the blow.

"Well, beautiful, I hope you're calling to tell me that you're going invite me up for a pre-dinner snack," Justin said upon answering.

Aubrey went into character quickly. "Hello, sweetie. I miss you so much, but unfortunately, I got caught up in a business meeting. I'm going to have to skip dinner, but will be ready for our night at the Kimmel Center. I promise, daddy."

Justin could not resist her sexy voice and her referring to him as "daddy" put him under a spell. "I guess I have no choice, beautiful. Take care of your business. I understand. We'll make up the time after the show."

Aubrey smiled. She was not trying to be exclusive with Justin so soon, but his sex was different than what she was used to. She actually enjoyed their time together.

"Okay, baby. See you about six-thirty."

The truth was Aubrey was not really into the culture scene. Sure, she had money, but she did not come from money. She was still a ghetto girl, which was one reason she became so upset with Brea when she called her a southern ghetto girl. Justin had no idea the girl that he was falling for was a pole dancing psycho who had made a portion of her fortune from playing johns from the club and the rest from Jerome's stash, which made her an instant millionaire.

Aubrey continued to read about Scottie and his success. She felt like a fool for brushing him off due to his appearance. Then she thought about Justin and how fine and well off he was, but she wanted to keep an open mind.

Aubrey started her car up, turned the GPS on, and programmed it to save travel routes. She put her car in gear and slowly pulled out of the parking spot, trying not to hit the gas too hard. Aubrey drove through the streets of Philadelphia until she could not hear the hustle and bustle of the city streets. The further she drove the more bare trees and long lawns she saw. The time melted away, and she did not realize she had been driving for about forty minutes. She saw a sign that read Welcome to Villanova, but she had no idea where she was. Aubrey drove around the block twice trying to remember the street she was on. After she gained her boundaries, she punched in the address to the Kimmel Center.

* * * * *

Justin placed his last cufflink through the buttonhole on his shirt, then gave himself the once over as he stood in front of his full-length mirror.

"Damn, I look good," he said with a devilish grin.

He could not wait to show up at Aubrey's door and see her light up at the sight of his sexiness. Justin was sexy and he knew it. However, he lacked the street swagger that Aubrey was used to.

Justin was dressed in all black. His classic tuxedo reflected his style and personality; it screamed class. He jazzed it up with an Armani black and white pinstripe shirt. Justin checked his Burberry watch, which reflected the cue that it was time to meet his beautiful date. Justin salivated at the thought of what sexy gown Aubrey would show up in. He loved her exotic look and more so her style to match. He was falling for her fast. The fact that she was independent made his admiration for her even greater.

Justin took one last gander in the mirror to be sure he was just right for Aubrey. Then he grabbed his key and the petite bouquet of roses sitting on his coffee table and headed out the door. Walking through the corridor, he waved at fellow pedestrians. The excitement of the night framed his face. He wore a grin bigger than life. A short walk and a few floors up on the elevator, and he was outside of Aubrey's door. He took a deep breath, nervous as if it were their first encounter. To Justin, it was just as important. This would be the night that he had a real date with Aubrey. He had experienced her body, but he was after her most intimate place...her heart.

Justin reached his right hand out as it formed a fist to make his presence known. Thump...thump...thump! The sound echoed in the hallway. He listened intently while breathing in Aubrey's intoxicating perfume that lingered softly in the air. His knocking yielded no response. Justin thumped the door again. This time, he placed his ear to the door and nothing. All that remained of Aubrey was the faint smell she had left behind. Confused, Justin looked at his watch and then his cell phone. He had no missed calls, but further investigation revealed a voice message.

"When did my phone ring? I hope she's not cancelling on me."

Justin reluctantly pressed the button on his cell phone to play the message and listened with full attention.

"Hello, Justin. I'm running a little later than planned. I will meet you before the curtain goes up. Can't wait to see you. I know you killin' that tux."

Justin was not happy about Aubrey being late, but her message, especially the ending, softened the blow. He ended his voicemail and placed a call to her phone. After about four rings, her voicemail came on, and he left her instructions on where and what.

* * * * *

Brooke made it home through rush-hour traffic just in time to see the news. She was a routine oriented person who had to see the news, even if it meant sitting through an hour of human tragedy. She needed to feel connected, and that was her way of keeping up with what was going on. She remembered her mother spending time watching the news daily. She always told Brooke that she should care about what's going on in the world.

Brooke made a few trips back to her vehicle to gather all of her bags. On her second trip, she turned on the television and tuned in to her local news station. This night was different. She wanted to see the segment on local entrepreneurs where Scottie was one of the featured stories.

The last bag was placed in the house, and Brooke collapsed on her white plush sofa. Enveloped in luxury, she let her body completely relax and sink deeper into the oversized pillows. She could see the Philadelphia skyline from her downtown piece of heaven.

Brooke began to smile at the thought of Scottie and her spending the day together. She really had a dilemma to handle with the Scottie and Brenson saga. She hated herself for crossing the line with Brenson and ruining any chances with a future with Scottie. More importantly, she wondered if Scottie even thought about her that way.

Her favorite commercial came on and took her mind away from the heavy thoughts briefly. She chuckled as she switched the channel. A restless Brooke tossed and propped her feet up on the coffee table. For some reason, she was not able to settle down. She scrolled through her cellphone messages as to cure her uneasy feeling. Then she gazed up at the stars that twinkled in her window. Up she jumped off of the sofa, finally giving into her body's yearning disguised as boredom. Brooke walked to the kitchen to get a glass of her favorite wine as she dialed her phone. She poured as she awaited Brenson's smooth voice to ooze through the phone's speaker.

"What's up, sexy. I've been waiting on your call. So are we on for dinner and dessert or..."

Brooke stopped him mid-sentence to gain control of the conversation. "Hello to you, too, Bren. And the answer to your question is yes. I'll be ready in about an hour. Where are we meeting?"

Brenson paused before answering her. "Let's meet at my place. You can leave your car, and I'll drive. Where I'm taking you is sort of a surprise."

"Okay. I'll see you in one hour."

After ending the call, Brooke hurried to smell and look as good as possible. She planned to enjoy their time together until it ended.

* * * * *

Aubrey hopped out of the car as she raced against time, hoping she had not missed out on the entire show. She also was terrified that Justin would be pissed with her. She had just started getting him where she wanted him and was not ready for him to have a bad taste concerning her in his mouth just yet. All the money she possessed and newfound place in the world was not enough. Aubrey believed in having a backup plan, and Justin was the star of her Plan B.

Aubrey stumbled through the dark auditorium, trying not to disturb others. She scanned the room to find Justin's handsome face. She had no luck, and people were starting to get annoyed. So, she excused herself and stepped into the hallway. As she stepped into the bright decorated space, Aubrey texted Justin, hoping to find out where their seats were. Justin responded to the text promptly, and Aubrey headed to the second level of the theater to the box seats. She felt silly that she did not know he had gotten them the best seats.

Aubrey arrived to the correct section of the theater to see Justin standing awaiting her arrival. He was a perfect picture, holding a petite bouquet of roses. Aubrey smiled as her heart skipped a beat. She had never felt that before. Justin's gestures never came off as corny to her; they genuinely were meant to make the other person feel good.

Justin handed Aubrey the flowers as his bright smile went dim. Aubrey had come to a downtown show wearing the same clothes she had worn to her business meeting, while everyone else was in formal attire. Justin did not make a fuss, though. There was only thirty minutes left of the performance, and he wanted to spend it happily.

* * * * *

Brooke stepped out of her sexy Mustang looking flawless. She went with the sexy, but practical look. The weather was still frigid and urged all those it came in contact with to cover up. Brooke sported a classic cream and gold tweed skirt with a twist. One side was long, and the other raised just enough to allow her right leg and knee-high boot to peek out at its hem. Six-inch chocolate brown boots framed her long legs. Her matching tailored tweed blazer with its peek-a-boo lace back sat perfectly over her leather bustier.

Brooke set her car alarm and proceeded to Brenson's place. Once at the door, she extended her left gloved hand out to ring his intercom.

"Who is it?" Brenson answered.

Brooke softly spoke back, "It's me, Bren. Open up. It's cold."

With no further words exchanged, the door buzzer sounded, and she entered the building. Brooke walked quickly to the elevator to get to Brenson's bachelor pad. By the time she reached her destination, the door was already cracked, awaiting her arrival. Brooke pushed the door completely open as she announced her presence. Her eyes were competing with her brain. What she saw was unreal.

"What's all of this?" she asked slowly with an unsure tone.

Brenson stood there like a proud parent showing off his newborn. "This is all for you...the surprise."

Brooke was amazed. Brenson's spacious loft had been turned into a five-star restaurant and spa all at once. The massive fireplace that anchored the living space had been turned into the backdrop of a spa for two. Massage tables, flowers, and an assortment of oils sat on the portable table next to the massage tables. Ten feet from the spa in front of his wall-to-wall window was a fully set table adorned with gold leaf china. Adjacent to the dining table was a large gold cart with gold dome serving stations and two attending chefs. Music played softly in the background to serve as the mood setter. Candles sat on what seemed like every surface. The illumination was beautiful throughout the home. Brooke knew she was in too deep. For the first time in a long time, she was speechless.

* * * * *

Justin and Aubrey walked hand in hand into the hotel talking about what Aubrey missed and how amazing the finale was. Aubrey leaned in and planted a kiss on Justin's soft lips, then urged him to follow her. She wanted to make up for being late. Justin smiled and followed her lead. He was excited just to be in her presence.

Justin and Aubrey made their way to the elevator. Aubrey was on super charge; she could not wait until she got to her penthouse. As the elevator doors closed, she clawed and kissed Justin. She was used to giving after receiving; it came natural to her. Justin loved to experience her body, too, but he did not want her to think that was all he wanted from her.

Justin guided her hands from his groin to his heart, while kissing her passionately. A dizzy Aubrey tried to gain her footing. Her entire body tingled. She stepped back to catch her breath.

"You felt that, too?" he asked her, speaking of the electric jolt between them.

Aubrey did not know how to feel real emotions. She only knew how to make others feel good. Quickly recovering, she grabbed for his crotch again.

"Yes, I felt it and it was big."

While kissing her again, Justin pressed the stop button on the elevator. Aubrey's eyes lit up. He's freakier than I thought. This just might work, she thought to herself.

Justin looked at her as he reached both hands out and placed them on her shoulders, turning Aubrey around so her back faced him. He pulled a handkerchief out of his right pocket, then placed it over her eyes.

"Aubrey, I have a surprise for you. Just trust me."

When she felt the elevator moving again, Aubrey was a little disappointed that he didn't ravish her right then and there.

A few more floors up, and the elevator stopped. Justin escorted Aubrey off of the elevator, being careful so she did not bump into the walls.

"Where are we, Justin?" Aubrey asked, reaching both hands out in front of her.

"Remember, Aubrey, no questions," he replied.

Justin opened the door to his suite and then removed the blindfold. As Aubrey opened her eyes, she saw a nicely furnished suite with a few extras, including a flat-screen television and separate spacious bedroom. Her first thought was that Justin wanted to get it on in a new room for the night, which was fine with her.

He then walked her over to the large window. Philadelphia as the background of the evening was beautiful. Justin and Aubrey stood wrapped in each other's arms, looking out the window in complete silence.

Aubrey finally said, "You brought me to a suite to get some sweets."

They both laughed. She continued fishing to find out his intentions.

"You could have had all of this in my penthouse. Why the change of scenery?"

Justin began to kiss Aubrey in between her words, using his hands to explore every inch of her body. He continued to explore Aubrey's body as he answered her questions.

"This is my place. I wanted you to see where I stay. It's important to me that you really know me."

Aubrey moved away seductively, trying not to appear obviously concerned.

Justin picked up on it and said, "What's wrong, sweetie? Was I hurting your arm?"

Aubrey gave him a fake smile. "No, I'm just thirsty and want to get a little more comfortable. Do you have any wine?"

Excusing himself, Justin went to retrieve the wine from his closet. He returned with a bottle of chardonnay and two glasses. As he poured the wine, Aubrey continued her questioning.

"So this is where you stay when you're working late or something?"

Justin turned around and proceeded to walk toward her with two full glasses of wine. Aubrey reached for one of the glasses.

"No, this is where I live. It's only me, and the board is free. You can't beat that. I save a lot of money and still get to live in luxury. It's the perfect situation."

Aubrey felt like a fool. She thought he was like part owner in the hotel or at least making that kind of money.

"Oh, I see. You save money on staying here, but you splurge on luxury cars. You got a little hood in you after all."

They both chuckled.

"I don't need to buy a car. I have free car service. I get to choose from various luxury cars on a daily basis. I make good money, but not to have four and five cars."

Aubrey's heart dropped in her stomach. Her dream Plan B had just turned into a nightmare. She had started to like Justin, but not enough to deal with his middle-class ass. She needed a baller to insure constant money flow, just in case something happened to her millions. She hated the fact that she fell for his charm and assumed he was rich.

"So what's good money?"

Justin looked at Aubrey with wide eyes. "Wow, Ms. Green. You're direct, huh?"

Aubrey was planning an exit strategy as Justin continued on.

"I'm just playing with you, Aubrey. I don't mind telling you. I make about three hundred thousand a year and about two hundred and fifty thousand after taxes. I've been here for about five years now and expect about three hundred and fifty thousand with bonuses this year."

Aubrey quickly lost interest. She knew she could spend that amount of money in a day on a large purchase. She stood up and looked at her phone.

"Justin, I had fun tonight, but I have to get up early for a meeting."

Justin had just experienced the cold shoulder. Aubrey kissed him on the cheek as she headed for the door.

Aubrey arrived to her room in one piece, but inside she felt broken. She had left her past life trying to reach a new one, and it was not starting off with a good record. She placed her key in the lock and turned the handle. Aubrey stormed into the penthouse and headed straight for the closet to gather some clothes and other items. Her anger brewed with each article of clothing she gathered. She had few clothes left to pack and move into her new place.

Her breathing sped up, and she began to yell to herself as if talking to another person. "You are so stupid! How could you not do your research? First, a fake publishing house pulled you in, and then you almost fell for this middle class working stiff! Nobody is who they seem to be. This day could not get any worse. But, they will pay for trying to trick me like Momma. That's for sure."

Aubrey quickly changed her clothes after she finished gathering clothes in a Gucci duffle bag. Armed with rage in her heart and determined to get reciprocity, she headed out of the door.

Her ride on the elevator seemed to take forever. She went over the plan in her mind repeatedly. Things seemed to be getting out of hand, and she hated not being in control. All of those years under Jerome's thumb coupled with living in the shadow of a selfish whoring mother had taken a toll on Aubrey. She was unstable and had no coping skills.

Aubrey made it to her car, where she opened the trunk and placed her bag inside. Then she hopped in the driver's seat and started on her journey. Aubrey struggled to power on her GPS and then searched for her destination in the database. She drove in complete silence while paying close attention to the roads traveled. The night air was ice cold and the fog became thicker as she descended into the wooded areas and away from the city lights. Her mind raced as she drove. She thought about how disrespectful she had been treated at LRP and how horrible Renee and Brea were about her story.

The sound of ringing bells chimed. She grabbed her purse with her right hand, while trying to keep the steering wheel steady with the left. Aubrey retrieved her phone and scanned the screen for a number or name before answering. Who is calling me, and so late? she thought to herself. When she saw Justin's name on the screen, she quickly hit the ignore call button. It was close to twelve o'clock in the morning, and she surely did not want to talk to him.

As she placed her phone on the armrest, her GPS alerted her that her destination was up ahead. Aubrey drove for another block and then pulled into a driveway that had a For Sale sign posted in the yard. Her phone text alert went off. She opened it up and began to read. The sender was Justin.

I went to your room and got no answer when I knocked. Where are you? We need to talk. Call me when you get this.

Aubrey looked at the text for a moment before turning her phone off. She then popped her trunk and threw her phone and purse inside. She was on a mission and did not need any distractions. After placing her key under her seat for a quick getaway, she put on her gloves on and headed toward her destination.

She walked briskly, as not to linger and risk being seen on the suburban street. Once she located the correct home, she put her plan into action. Dressed in all black, which would make it hard for someone to see her in the dark, Aubrey approached the well-manicured lawn. The big single home was far enough from the next house to allow for privacy. To Aubrey's surprise, a light was still on in the center of the house.

"Oh, I see I have a night owl on my hands," she said aloud.

Aubrey quickly changed her plans. Having not imagined her being woke at this time of night, she didn't want to risk her hearing the lock being picked and call the cops. Slowly, Aubrey made her way to midway in the driveway. While squatting down next to a black Tahoe, she shook the handle to set the alarm off. Aubrey peaked around the driver's side, searching for any movement inside the house. Aubrey saw one shadow and then another in the upstairs window. The alarm stopped and both shadows disappeared. Aubrey gave the truck another strong shove before retreating to the bushes near the front door. She knew this time someone would come out to see what was going on.

She had to think quickly on her feet. There were two people inside the house, when she had only expected one. She checked her waist pouch for her tools.

"Now I have to change plans again," she whispered. Just as she suspected, the lock on the front door turned and she heard a man's voice.

"Sweetie, I'll be right back. No need to follow me. I'm sure it's those damn deer. I don't know why you always park in the driveway when we have a two-car garage. I'll pull it in the garage so I can get some sleep around here."

The tall, dark-skinned man pointed the keypad at the door, and Aubrey heard the garage door open. The man walked out, leaving the door cracked. When he got closer to the truck, Aubrey slipped in the house. Her eyes scanned the area quickly looking for somewhere she could hide. She had only brought enough "fun juice" for one person, so now she had to think fast. Aubrey hid behind a large cabinet in the living room. A few minutes later, she heard the front door close and the lock turn. Then she saw the lights go out in the living room and heard the man stumble over items in the hallway.

"Good night, baby. The car is in the garage. Don't stay up too late."

"I won't," a female voice assured him.

Aubrey competed with her mind and body to remain completely still. She remained out of sight for about twenty minutes. Sounds of soft music escaped from a spacious room adjacent to the living room. When Aubrey thought the coast was clear, she walked gently across the plush carpeted floor until she reached the stairs. Although she was careful to be gentle on each step, she heard a loud crack when she got halfway up the stairs.

From the room downstairs, she heard the woman call out, "Phil, are you still up? Phil?"

Aubrey quickly ran up the rest of the stairs and headed straight to the front room. To her surprise, the bed was empty and Phil was coming out of the bathroom. He was flabbergasted.

"Who the hell..."

His words were cut short by Aubrey leaping forward. Before he could say another word, she stabbed him in the neck with a syringe filled with Barbital and two other perfectly mixed tranquilizers. Phil fell to the bed as he was rendered unconscious. Although he hit the bed, it was a muffled thump sound that traveled through the room. Aubrey quickly hid when she heard footsteps on the stairs.

Brea entered the room to find her husband halfway on the bed and non-responsive, but breathing. Quickly, she turned to retrieve the phone to call an ambulance. That's when Aubrey stepped out of the shadows holding a .380 caliber handgun complete with silencer and stood in front of her. Brea's eyes grew large as saucers. She opened her mouth, but no sound came out.

"Hello, Mrs. Tillman," Aubrey said with a devilish grin.

Brea's eyes flooded with tears, but she still couldn't speak.

"Oh, now the cat got your tongue. What happened to all of the fake criticism you gave me earlier?"

Brea finally found her voice. "What do you want? I will give it to you. Just leave me and my husband alone. Please, please. I'm sorry for the..."

Aubrey placed the silencer to Brea's right temple. "Listen to me. You will not speak unless asked to, or I will end this quickly. Now, let's go."

She pointed the gun, gesturing for Brea to go into the bathroom. Now crying hysterically, Brea did not know what to expect, but she knew it wouldn't be good. Aubrey ordered her to place the drain stopper in the tub and turn on the water. While bent over the tub, Brea tried to think of a way out. She gained some courage and attempted to preserve her life. Brea came up from bending over the tub and hit Aubrey in the head full force with a can of shaving cream. Aubrey stumbled backwards and almost fell into the sink. Brea attempted to escape from the bathroom, but a dazed Aubrey gained her footing and grabbed Brea by the back of the head. She spit fire.

"Bitch, no you didn't! Now you're gonna really pay!"

Aubrey smacked Brea in the head several times with the gun, and Brea fell to the floor unconscious. Aubrey paced the floor trying to gain her full senses back.

When Brea awoke, she hoped it had all been a bad dream. However, as she adjusted her eyes, she saw Aubrey sitting in front of her with the gun pointed directly at her. Brea was fully dressed and submerged in a bathtub full of water.

"You're back with us. Welcome back, Mrs. Tillman," Aubrey said sarcastically.

Still groggy, Brea yelled, "You sick bitch! What are you doing to me? What have I done so bad for you to break into my house and torture me?"

Aubrey sat back in her chair and gave a look of assurance. "I'm not going to torture you. Just sit back and listen."

She unfolded a piece of paper with typewritten words on it and prepared to read.

"Page forty of Southern Sassy explains it all, but if you would have actually read it instead of skimming it, and then embarrassing me at the meeting, you would know what's happening." Aubrey crossed her legs and continued. "Here it goes..."

"Sassy was broken in her spirit. She endured more abuse than anybody should have in a lifetime. Her mother used her and disregarded her feelings. She had nothing left to give her. Their relationship was tainted like a blood-stained bandage. She knew if she did nothing, she would remain in this hell forever. Sassy entered the bathroom as her mother lay soaking, getting ready for yet another date."

She paused and looked at Brea. Now trembling, Brea did not want to know what was next in the story.

"See, Mrs. Tillman. Sassy gained strength earlier on in the story. You should have read it before you offended me. See, she was not weak as her mother thought. And my 'Cat in the Hat' book is not a nursery rhyme after all."

She stood up, folded the paper, and placed it back into her waist pouch. Brea breathed a sigh of relief when she saw Aubrey preparing to leave. Aubrey walked toward the vanity and sink, where she stopped to look at her reflection in the mirror. Aubrey talked to Brea while looking at her reflection.

"I told you that I wasn't going to torture you."

Brea attempted to get up from the tub, but was too weak. As she closely watched Aubrey rubbing her hair, she asked, "So what are you going to do with me? I won't tell anyone about this. I swear."

Aubrey turned to face Brea with a calm look. "I know you won't...because I'm going to kill you."

Just as the last syllable escaped her lips, Aubrey grabbed the hair dryer that was plugged in the outlet, turned it on, and tossed it in the bath water. Then she turned and walked out as the lights in the bathroom flickered.

Chapter 12

Homecoming

Spice awoke to her neighbor in the adjacent cell yelling and pleading to make a phone call. She did not know how much longer she would be able to endure the horrific conditions of lockup. Metta, Spice's cellie, was sound asleep. Unlike Spice, she had grown accustomed to the loud, unpredictable environment.

Spice placed one foot at a time out of her bed. In an almost paralyzed state, she looked in the corner of her cell. There sat the toilet that she made her morning starter every day since being placed in the shit hole. Privacy was a distant memory, and this fact was breaking Spice down. She hated how she felt inside having to use the toilet and everything else with an audience.

She climbed out of bed, sliding her right foot and then left against the concrete floor. This day seemed a little more problematic. Her body ached from the impromptu beatings that she received from inmates orchestrated by Officer Truman. Her latest beating was served in the shower with a bar of soap in a sock less than twenty-four hours prior. Spice was sore all over and had bruises to match. Several attempts to see the social worker failed. Requests she placed in the social service box on the unit somehow disappeared every time.

Head in hand, Spice sobbed uncontrollably as feelings of brokenness consumed her. Depression festering deep in her belly left her wanting to hear a familiar voice; anybody that knew her would be fine. Thoughts of ending it all were a daily struggle for Spice. She was alone in a place that did nothing but cause her pain.

Spice pulled her orange jumpsuit down and mounted the stainless steel throne. Tears continued to flow as she scanned her cortex for memories from home that may give her the strength to hold on.

* * * * *

The night turned from pitch black to the sun struggling to make its appearance through the clouds. Aubrey switched gears as she weaved between two cars. Her eyes were heavy, and the sunlight made her squint. She reached down to grab her phone, which had been ringing all night. Justin would not let up, despite her sending him to voicemail with each call.

Without checking the number, she answered with a shout. "Yes! Who is this?"

To her surprise, a female's voice spoke from the other end. "Hello. This is Allona. Jimmy gave your number to me. He had to step out, but he wanted me to find out how long it would be before you get here."

Aubrey opened the window to let the brisk air hit her face. She needed to stay awake just a little longer.

She cleared her throat and said, "Allona, I don't know why Jimmy would have you call me. He knows how I feel about newcomers. I will call him when I'm close."

Aubrey hung up the phone and proceeded in her travels. Her GPS alerted her of the next turn, and she pulled up in a long driveway made of stone. The driveway seemed to be forever.

"Damn, I hate these rocks. I betta not get a flat!" Aubrey yelled.

She could see the curtains in the living room open and close. Aubrey made it to the house safely with her tires unscathed. She put her car in park and proceeded to the front door. The single-family brick house sat on a dirt road with miles of open space around it. Aubrey approached the red door and used the wooden door knocker to announce her arrival. A few seconds passed before the door opened with a creaking sound, just enough for Aubrey to enter. Aubrey stepped in the house and walked a few feet. She could smell food cooking on the stove and hear the static from the radio.

"Jimmy, where you are?"

Just as she said the last word, someone approached her from behind and with a trembling hand placed a gun barrel to her head.

A soft voice with a slight country drawl asked, "Who are you, and how do you know Jimmy?"

Aubrey stood very still as she responded, "Allona, I suppose. I'm Aubrey."

Allona dropped her hand that held the gun. "Oh, I'm so sorry I thought you were going to call first. You can never be too cautious. Let me get Jimmy. He's upstairs in the lab."

Aubrey rubbed the back of her head as she stood in the living room awaiting Jimmy's arrival. Still shaken up, she continued to stand as she looked around at the changes that Jimmy had made since she last was in his domain. She heard heavy footsteps getting closer. As Jimmy turned the corner, Aubrey had to close her mouth to keep from salivating. Jimmy approached her and lifted her up off of her feet.

"Hey, sexy lady, you still looking good," he said as he placed her back on her feet.

Aubrey leaned back to do a double take. "I see you're looking well yourself. I also see you couldn't forget about me, so you found yourself a cheap knock off...with a name that begins with an 'A' and all."

Jimmy looked back to see where Allona was and make sure she hadn't overhead Aubrey. Laughing, he replied, "Don't get messed up in here. She has your fire, too."

Aubrey laughed as not to feel uncomfortable. Jimmy and Aubrey had a past together that did not turn out so great, but they remained in contact for business when needed.

"Okay, let's get down to business," Aubrey continued. "Do you have what I need?"

Jimmy gave her a quick look and then walked over to his stash spot. He was the man on the south end and had his hands in everything crooked that one could imagine.

"Okay, Bre, stand over here and smile. I need to do a test run."

Aubrey did as she was told. She trusted Jimmy because she knew he was the best at what he did. While looking through the test photos, Jimmy confirmed it was good to go.

"Aubrey, Allona will sew this on your head, and I need you to put these on before we do a real shot."

While watching Jimmy intently, she wished his six-foot, six-inch muscular frame was all over her. Jimmy handed Aubrey a bag with all of the items that she requested, and the process began.

* * * * *

Detective Torrey sat at his desk with his headphones on. He loved to listen to the oldies while working; it cleared his head and gave him a feeling of peace. Seeing the horrible things that plagued the world day in and day out made him appreciate the small things in life, like music. He shifted through the papers on his desk that were piled up from cases he had the responsibility of solving.

The red button on his phone lit up, alerting him that he had voice messages. He was awaiting a call from the crime lab with a hunch that he had about Jerome's murder case. Detective Torrey checked his voicemail and muddled through them, hoping the lab results were in. He was just about to hang up, when he was alerted that he had one more message. Detective Torrey leaned back in his chair and listened carefully. The message was from Atlanta Medical Center.

"Detective Torrey, this is the laboratory at Atlanta Medical Center. We sent results of a patient's rape kit to your office, but they were returned undeliverable. The envelope had the wrong address. I apologize for the mix-up. These results are weeks old. I need you to contact our lab immediately if you are still the officer on the case. Once again, I apologize, as we are not allowed to give this information over the phone."

Detective Torrey hung up disappointed; still no word from the police crime lab. He had plenty of cases and did not know offhand of any rape cases on his desk. Detective Torrey looked through all of his files and attempted to locate any victim taken to Atlanta Medical. His eyes grew wide when he saw it on his computer screen. The second victim from his most important case was still at Atlanta Medical. Only she had not been raped, but brought in as a gunshot patient. Detective Torrey anxiously dialed the phone number listed on the screen and waited for an answer.

* * * * *

The lobby inside of the busy Atlanta prison was filled with people from wall to wall. Mothers, sons, daughters, aunts, and uncles were all in line to bring their loved ones some comfort during their stay behind bars. The line seemed never ending as frustration levels reached an all-time high. A young lady in the front of the line caused a problem and had to be escorted out of the building. She was dressed in attire that resembled a raunchy streetwalker. The lady screamed and kicked as the officers escorted her to the front doors. The dress codes for visitors were pointed out to her before she went off, but still, she went on and on about how she drove twenty-five miles to come visit and how ghetto the jail was for handling their guests that way. The procedure was clear to most normal people: dress modestly, sign in, present identification, and have a seat until your name was called. The officers laughed and imitated the irate would-be visitor.

A tall male officer with blonde hair stepped forward and yelled over the noisy lobby, "Martise Watkins! Martise Watkins, please step forward."

An exotic-looking girl came forward. She resembled a biracial woman most likely of Indian decent. She had chestnut brown hair that swept across her shoulder with cascading curls. As the women stepped up, the officer took a deep breath.

"Hello, ma'am. Here is your identification. Please leave any personal belongings in one of the lockers in the lobby. Once you have placed your belongings safely in the locker, step to your left, please, and follow the officer."

She walked away as the entire group of officers stared at her perfect shape. Martise followed the directions given to her and returned to the officer's station. She was then escorted to a secluded room to the left of the check-in counter. A female officer with strong, manly hands gave her directions on what to remove and where to stand. The officer strip searched Martise, checking every hiding place. Once Martise cleared the strip search, she was escorted to the visitation area.

The steel door opened, and inmates dressed in orange jumpsuits entered in a steady stream. A husky female officer walked in the room behind them, and the male officer on duty gave her a head nod. Shortly thereafter, a confused Spice entered the room scanning the area for a familiar face. Hours prior, she had questioned her reason for living, and now she had a visitor.

The attending guard escorted Spice to the booth where her visitor waited. Spice approached with caution, but did not let on that she did not recognize the woman. Officer Truman shot her a look, and Spice lowered her head.

"Sit down, Dorsey, or be escorted back to your cell," the burly officer commanded.

Spice followed her directions and sat slowly while attempting to endure the soreness in her body. Eyeballing Spice's visitor, Officer Truman gave her a wink. She smiled back.

Now seated, Spice picked up the black phone and whispered, "Okay, who are you? Please tell me that you're here to save me." Spice looked at her closely, trying to find a familiar soul.

"It's me, Spice...Bre."

Spice did a double-take. She stared into the woman's chestnut brown eyes. Then it hit her. "Oh my God, what the hell happened? But your eyes are grey and hair black. How did you know I was here? You weren't at the club for a couple of days before I got knocked, and..."

Aubrey stopped her before she said too much. She had to make Spice think she was on her side.

"I saw it on the news, and a few of the girls told me how you got caught up in this craziness. I know you loved Jerome, so this can't be true!"

Spice breathed a sigh of relief. "Finally, someone who believes me. I've been so lonely in here, Bre, and the treatment I've been receiving is horrible."

Aubrey nodded and replied, "I can see somebody did a number on you. I was sent here by Jerome's right-hand man, Clark, to check and be sure you're safe. I was given money to put on your books and assigned the task of getting you a lawyer and all."

Spice began to cry and smile at the same time. She thought about how she was just ready to check out, and now an unlikely helper had been sent her way. Spice leaned in close enough to the glass to kiss it.

"Bre, please get me out of here. I know we were not close in the past because I thought you were going after Jerome, but now I see that I can trust you. You went through all of this for me, getting disguised and everything. I am so grateful."

Aubrey gave Spice a sincere look. "Listen to me. I got your back. Now, I need you to hear me. I know you're being mistreated and beaten in here. Who is doing this to you?"

Having gained her trust, Aubrey was now playing her like a fiddle. Spice's eyes scanned the room and landed on Officer Truman. Just then, the announcement was made by the male officer that only five minutes remained for the visits. Aubrey understood Spice's eye contact and nodded her head. Aubrey reassured Spice of her intentions.

"Spice, I have to go, but just know that I do not believe you killed Jerome and Quanda for one minute."

Confused, Spice gave Aubrey a strange look. "You don't know about Quanda?"

Aubrey squinted her eyes as if to say, What?

"One more minute!" the officer shouted.

Aubrey was distracted by the movement and sudden raise in volume inside the room.

"What about Quanda?" Aubrey asked.

Seeing Officer Truman on her way to personally end Spice's session, Spice spoke softly and quickly. "Quanda did not die, thank God. She's in the hospital in and out of consciousness, but not able to speak at all. I hope she gets up for good and able to clear my name."

Officer Truman tapped Spice on the shoulder. Spice said goodbye and then dropped the phone.

Aubrey felt like she had just been hit by a Mack truck. For the first time since she murdered Jerome, she did not feel safe. Aubrey dropped the phone receiver, stood to her feet, and turned to walk away. She took three steps before turning back around to catch Officer Truman eyeballing her. Despite the snag in her day, she had to follow through with her plan. Aubrey waved and winked at Officer Truman before being escorted through the jail to the lobby.

Aubrey made it back to where she started, still thinking about what Spice had said during the end of their visit. The lobby was thin and visitations were over for the day. People hurried to the lockers to collect their items and make the next bus leaving the area. Aubrey walked through the sparse lobby still the center of attention.

"Quanda is alive," she said to herself. "This is not good. I got to go to Plan C."

Aubrey gathered her belongings out of the rented locker, and while taking her time to place her jewelry back on, she pretended to make a couple of phone calls then took out her pen and pad. She adjusted her tea-length wool skirt that hugged her hips and bottom just right. Her black boots clicked against the tile floor with her slow walk. She noticed that officers were relieving each other for the lunch break for second shift, so she lingered around in the lobby. She was sure she would have a visitor soon and wanted to play her part. Aubrey looked at her watch, giving her plan a few more minutes. She was a good reader of personalities, and she always knew when someone was interested in her. However, she started to second guess her skills.

Just as she placed her faux fur waist-length jacket on and began to zip it up, she spotted Officer Truman walking out into the lobby. When Officer Truman stopped to talk to her fellow officers, Aubrey acted as though she had not seen her and disappeared into the bathroom located in the corner of the lobby. Officer Truman played her game. She continued to talk to her fellow officers before explaining she needed to go to the restroom before leaving for break. Before she could walk away from them, a couple of the officers gave Officer Truman a list of items to bring back from the store.

Officer Truman entered the restroom, and there Aubrey stood leaning against the sink while washing her hands. Officer Truman brushed past her to test the waters.

"You're still here? I thought you would have been gone."

Aubrey turned around and stared the officer in her eyes as she fluttered her long lashes.

"If I knew you were so bad at this cat and mouse game, I would have been gone home."

Officer Truman stared into her pretty chestnut eyes, courtesy of Jimmy. Aubrey could read the officer's need to be in control, so she played that up. Officer Truman continued to flirt.

"Was all of your waving and winking upstairs for me?"

Aubrey smiled and brushed back up against the officer. Then she grabbed her by the collar and led her inside the largest stall. Officer Truman looked around to be sure no one else was in the restroom. Once in the stall, Aubrey leaned against the wall. Overtaken by lust, Officer Truman got off on thinking that she would make Aubrey her subordinate.

"Lift your skirt up, pretty lady."

Aubrey gave her what she wanted, doe eyes and all. The officer came closer and placed her hand on Aubrey's crotch to find a soaking wet pair of lace panties. Aubrey moaned as she took herself back to the days of performing on stage. Aubrey was all alone in her mind, pleasuring herself. She arched her back and gyrated on the officer's hand with a low, steady motion.

Officer Truman was in her own fantasy, having public sex with a smoking hot girl while she was in control. She pulled her hand out and smelled Aubrey's juices. The smell of pheromones and pink chiffon body spray lingered on her nose hairs. Aubrey fondling her own nipples and still moaning turned her on even more.

The officer knew she only had a short break, but could not resist tasting Aubrey just for a few minutes. She did not expect Aubrey to taste so good. Officer Truman planted one knee on the cold floor of the restroom, pulled Aubrey's body close to her, and gave long, slow licks in her wet spot from back to front. In between slurps, she talked about how she had thought about tasting her when she first saw her. Aubrey squirted back to back in a matter of minutes.

The restroom door opened, and they both fought to remain still. In rushed someone who went into the stall closest to the door. High off of Aubrey's juices, Officer Truman found it hard to bring her sexual energy down. After they heard the door close once the person had exited, Aubrey slipped out of the stall first, but not before slipping Officer Truman a handwritten note.

* * * * *

The phone rang three times, and Detective Torrey waited anxiously. A voice came through the speaker on the phone.

"Atlanta Medical, Hector speaking. How may I help you?"

"Hello. My name is Detective Torrey, and I received a message from your lab about results from a rape kit. Do you know who the kit was done on and the results?"

The lab tech paused before responding, "We cannot give those answers over the phone, but we have everything ready for you. John called you, but he has already left for the day. We are open until eight o'clock this evening if you want to pick up everything and get the results in person."

Detective Torrey was frustrated but needed this information.

"Well, who are the results for? I have to be sure I'm not wasting my time."

"The name cannot be given over the phone, but I will tell you the initials are Q.R."

Detective Torrey looked at the name on his file, and sure enough those were Quanda's initials.

"Okay, Hector, I will be there before you close."

* * * * *

Aubrey spent the next hour searching hospitals in Atlanta for Quanda's unconscious body. She called over a dozen hospitals asking to be put through to her room. She finally found her after a tireless search at Atlanta Medical. She raced to make it before visiting hours were over. Aubrey was desperate, and she attempted to calm herself down as not to make stupid mistakes. She thought her plan out and hoped it went smoothly. She searched through her bag of goodies that Jimmy provided her with to see what she may need during her visit with Quanda.

Unsure of what to expect when she entered Quanda's room, she was consumed with fear. She knew that Quanda's existence, even if unconscious, posed a big threat for her. She ran the risk of her awakening fully and actually giving her name up.

Aubrey crossed the light as it turned from yellow to red. She pressed the button on her radio to change the channel as she tried to take her mind off of her task at hand. While pulling into the parking lot, the smooth music playing through the speakers took her away. She sang along with Trey Songz "I Can't Get Enough of You". Aubrey had not really experienced love, especially of this magnitude as explained in Trey's lyrics, but she used music to inspire her writing.

Aubrey briefly looked down at her writing pad, which was now filled with all new ideas that she jotted down as she experienced new things. Aubrey's wounds from rejection were still fresh, and taking Brea out merely put a Band-Aid on them. Brea's harsh criticism took her back to a place with her mother and her constant rejection and criticism.

Caught up in deep thought, she had to slam on her brakes quickly. A tall gentleman dressed in a blue suit and tie almost met his maker. As the man spun to the left, his coat flew open, exposing a black gun holster. Their eyes met, and Aubrey beeped her horn more out of fear than anything. She mouthed the words, Sorry, sir. The man acknowledged her apology with a nod as he pointed to the speed limit sign anchored on the metal pole.

Shaking and still putting a plan together, Aubrey pulled into a parking spot extremely slow. Overcorrecting her near accident, she took extra time to straighten her car perfectly.

Aubrey checked both side mirrors and rearview mirror before exiting her vehicle. Then she was off to handle business.

Aubrey went over the final plans in her head. She parked close to the door to have a better chance at a fast getaway. Approaching the automatic doors, she spotted the back of the would-be victim. Aubrey lingered until the man could be seen no more. She checked her watch to be sure of the time. The automatic doors opened, and she entered the building. The lobby was filled with people. White coats and scrubs could be seen for more than thirty feet. Aubrey observed the flow of the information desk as visitors checked in and departed. There were many last-minute visitors trying to get in before the end of visiting hours. Aubrey had already called the hospital posing as a concerned out-of-town friend to get information on the floor and room number that Quanda resided in.

She slowly approached the desk. "Hello. I'm here to visit Maria Hernandez. She's a good friend of mine," she told the guard, then added, "I hate to see her in the hospital after all this time."

The guard checked the list of patients in his computer. As he scrolled down, he had a look of concern. After an extensive search, he looked up at Aubrey. "Sorry, ma'am, we don't have a Maria Hernandez here. Are you sure you have the right hospital?"

Aubrey smiled and leaned forward, exposing her cleavage. "I know she was married a while ago, so she may be listed under her married name."

Aubrey swept her hair behind her right ear, while looking directly in the guard's eyes. When the guard smiled back, she went in for the kill.

Leaning over the desk just enough to see the list of patients whose first names was Maria, she continued. "Officer Billings, is it? Let me call her sister. I traveled a while to get here, so I definitely want to get in before visiting hours are over."

Aubrey stepped away with her cell phone in hand, pretending to call a lifeline.

"Maria Wilson is the name she goes by," she told him upon returning to his desk.

The guard smiled. "Okay then. That makes sense. She's on the fourth floor, north wing. I just need identification, and you can sign in on the visitor's log."

Aubrey eagerly reached in her waist pouch and pulled out her identification, handing it to the guard.

"Martise, huh? Pretty name," the guard flirted with Aubrey as he printed out her visitor's pass.

Aubrey gave him a seductive glare and said, "Thanks." Then she placed her fake ID back in her pouch and headed to seal her freedom.

* * * * *

Detective Torrey made it to the lab just in time. The glass window in the center of the room gave a brief peak into the testing area. He was frustrated and a little pissed off about the check-in process. He had to sign in first before being allowed to enter the lab located in a special area. Then he had to show every form of ID except his social security card. Detective Torrey tapped on the window as the desk was not occupied.

"Hello! Hello!" he yelled through the small hole in the glass.

A short, heavyset man with glasses came to the window after a few more knocks. "Hello, can I help you?"

Detective Torrey took a deep breath and showed his badge. "Yes, I'm here to get information on test results for a patient."

The man held his right hand up with his index finger extended. "One minute, please."

He watched as the man walked to the back and pushed a cleaning cart further back. Detective Torrey leaned on the counter and looked through his cell phone impatiently. A minute or two later, an average height white man with red hair approached the window.

"Hello, how may I help you, sir?"

Detective Torrey sighed again. "I received a call from a fellow named Hector..."

The man cut him off. "Detective Torrey?" he said, more as a question than statement. "I'm Hector. We spoke earlier. I have information about a patient who came to the hospital connected with a crime. We sent the rape kit to you promptly, but it was returned. So, we tested it ourselves due to the mistake. This was done by a new technician, and it had the wrong address. Anyway, all I need is your ID and badge number to release the information."

Detective Torrey gathered his identification and handed it over. "Hector, can I ask you a question? Why did the hospital test the rape kit? Our crime lab usually handles that, and I did not order a rape kit. The victim came in from a murder and attempted murder scene."

While Hector gathered the papers with the results of the test, he continued his explanation. "The female patient arrived naked, and her vagina had visible secretions that appeared to be semen. The decision to test her was the call of the attending doctor. Swabs of her mouth, anus, vagina, nostrils, and ears were collected, as well as samples from under her nails."

The loud sound of papers crumpling echoed through the small hole in the glass. Hector gathered a small bag and a clear bag resembling a Ziploc bag that contained papers. Detective Torrey salivated as the items touched his hands. He hoped for the missing piece. Detective Torrey's hands shook as he separated the edges on the Ziploc bag. He removed the contents and could not believe his eyes. As he read the report, it was not what he expected at all.

Patient Quanda Randell: Vaginal tearing and anal penetration confirmed. DNA of a male found under fingernails on right hand. Mouth swab confirmed semen DNA match from fingernails of right hand and secretion from a female. DNA matching female secretions under left index finger...

Detective Torrey gasped for air. He thought to himself, I've just been handed a goldmine. Now all I have to do is get the crime lab to run this DNA against Jerome's and Cindy's DNA to seal the deal.

Detective Torrey walked toward the elevators. He knew if the DNA matched Cindy, he would have to change his theory of her catching Jerome and Quanda in the act. That would mean she was a willing participant.

* * * * *

Aubrey bypassed the 4th floor and got off of the elevator on the 6th floor instead. The doors of the elevator opened, and she stepped off as doctors and nurses ran to a code. She quickly began to scan the area to find room 676. She passed a food cart filled with dirty trays and other large equipment in the hallway. She was two rooms away, and her anxiety took over. She began to breathe quickly, and her eyes grew wide. Aubrey did not know what to expect upon entering the room. As Aubrey walked into the room, she was almost knocked over by the nurse who was leaving from taking Quanda's vitals and rotating her.

"Oh goodness, I am so sorry," the nurse said. "I did not see you, ma'am."

Aubrey helped her pick up her items from the floor. "No problem. I wasn't looking, either."

The nurse continued. "Hi, I'm her evening nurse. It's so nice that she has a visitor. You are the first one to come see her since her one and only visit from her children and social worker. Such a shame...what monster would do such a thing to such a beautiful woman?"

Aubrey gave a half smile, annoyed at the nerve of the nurse. She never exchanged words. The nurse felt the chill in the air and proceeded.

"Okay, I'm just rambling on. I will leave you to your visit. You only have a little time before visiting hours are over."

Aubrey turned her back to her and said, "Thanks. That sounds good."

There Quanda lay motionless. It seemed as if tubes were going in every hole of her body. The loud beeping sounds distracted Aubrey as she stared at her friend turned foe. Aubrey circled her bed as she became increasingly angry. Memories of the night that Quanda betrayed her flooded her memory banks. She continued to walk while chanting under her breath.

"You betrayed me. You betrayed me. You have to pay. All I wanted was out of that hell hole. "A single tear fell from Aubrey's right eye and onto the collar of her shirt. "She has to die," Aubrey rationalized with herself.

Now on the phone, the nurse watched Aubrey's odd behavior from the nurse's station. After ending her call, the nurse proceeded to check on her patient who was in the room adjacent to Quanda's.

Aubrey leaned over Quanda, who looked as if she were sleeping. While pretending to be showing Quanda an act of affection, Aubrey slipped one full syringe from her waist pouch. She then whispered in her ear as she stuck the syringe deep in the base of her neck.

"See you in hell, bitch." Aubrey squeezed the syringe until empty.

The alarm at the nurse's station chimed to alert the nurse that a patient needed assistance. Coming out of the patient's room, the nurse heard the alert. As she got closer to the desk, she realized the alert was coming from Quanda's room. The nurse quickly responded to the call. As she entered Quanda's room, she found Quanda alone with the call button taped to her hand and all of her monitors beeping as a flat line floated across the monitor.

Just then, Aubrey cracked open the bathroom door. As the nurse turned to run to the station and call a code, she was met with the same lethal cocktail when Aubrey shoved a filled syringe into her side.

"Next time, bitch, keep your opinions to yourself. Oh, wait. There won't be a next time."

The nurse fell to the floor and began foaming at the mouth. Aubrey turned to escape, only to be met by the security guard from the front desk. Quickly taking in the scene, he immediately tackled her to the ground. Aubrey kicked and struggled to get free. Thinking quickly, she pretended to surrender. While trying to keep her still, the guard lay on top of her and reached for his walkie-talkie. Aubrey waited until he reached halfway around his body. Then she delivered a swift knee to his scrotum. His walkie-talkie flew across the room and landed on the opposite side of bed. The guard fell over in pain yelling.

Now free and desperate to shut him up, Aubrey pulled out a six-inch blade and shoved it into his trachea. The room fell silent as blood escaped his body like a raging sea. Aubrey ran out of the room, heading for the stairway with her brown hair blowing in the wind. She knocked over the cart of trays in the hallway.

* * * * *

Detective Torrey made it back to the station. He could not wait to get the results of the test and have the new evidence ran against the DNA in the system. He walked briskly toward the lab. The double doors opened, and he proceeded to log in the evidence and fill out the paperwork for the appropriate testing. Just as he finished up his request, his phone alerted him of a missed call. While attempting to check his call log, the phone began ringing again.

"Detective Torrey speaking," he answered.

He listened to the voice on the other end and could not believe his ears.

"What? Homicide? Three bodies? I'm on my way now!" Detective Torrey hung up the phone and headed back to Atlanta Medical. Now his case just got real interesting.

* * * * *

Officer Truman thought about the encounter she had with Aubrey for the rest of her shift. She sat back on the unit as she enjoyed the quiet time. The prisoners were down on restricted movement, and her shift would soon be over. She decided to take out the note Aubrey had given her and read it for the fifth time. Officer Truman was truly smitten with who she believed to be Martise. She could not believe the contents of the letter.

She whispered to herself, "All this time that little bitch acted like she was better than me, and she was gay all along. And to threaten me."

The letter in her hand trembled. Officer Truman was furious and hated to have to hide how she really felt. She fixated her eyes on the yellow-lined paper.

Dear Officer,

I noticed you from the moment I walked in. I had to ignore you somewhat because my girl is very jealous. She and I have a past. That's the only reason I came to see her. I don't know why I'm telling you all of this. I feel so foolish. I do know you can't tell her about this letter. She has people that she will send to kill me if she knew I was telling you about us. I really want to get to know you, but it has to be a secret. Cindy told me that you get people to beat up on her and that she was going to get you in trouble. She wants me to tell the news and your superiors. I don't have much time before she checks to be sure I followed her commands. I hate being connected to her, but she has a lot of dirt on me. I know you probably think I'm crazy for telling you all of this, but I'm scared and have no one else to turn to. I have to find a way out of this shit. If you want to see me, call me at this number: 267 667-8903.

Officer Truman sat there contemplating her next move as she read the last words: On the run...

Aubrey's phone continued to ring nonstop. She had left Philly in the wee hours of the morning almost twenty-four hours prior. She was out of control and hated that feeling. Aubrey cried as she drove through the streets of Atlanta, attempting to calculate her next move. With a trail of bodies in her path, she was not able to concentrate. She did not plan on killing anyone. Feeling her hand was forced, the body count was sure to continue to add up.

Aubrey turned down a little street to be out of view. She exited the car carrying a spare license plate in her right-gloved hand and bent down to replace her tag. Wiping each eye, she attempted to get her vision together. All of her crying had started to dry her contacts out. Aubrey completed her task quickly, disposing of the dummy license plate and hopping back in the driver's side. Searching through the bag she got from Jimmy, attempting to locate the contact refreshing solution, distracted her attention away from her surroundings.

Aubrey's phone rang again, this time another unknown number. Feeling the pressure and sick of the bothersome calls, Aubrey picked up the phone ready to give Justin a piece of her mind.

"Justin, what the hell do you keep calling me for?"

There was a brief silence before the voice on the other end startled her.

"Bre? Bre, is that you? Oh lawdie, it is you. I've been so worried bout you. Who's Justin?"

Aubrey's tears flowed freely. The voice on the other end of the phone was that of her grandmother. She had not seen or heard from Aubrey in over a month and a half.

Paranoid, Aubrey quickly questioned her. "Granny, how did you get this number? This is a brand-new phone."

"Gal, what difference does it make? Are you okay? I've been worried sick about ya. I got a hang-up call from this number about two days ago. You pranking your old Granny?"

Aubrey laughed through her pain and tears. "No, Granny, it's no problem. I forgot that I called you. What are you doing up so late?"

"Gal, you know me. I'm a night owl. I just couldn't rest since I got that call. I'm so glad I pressed on and called the numba back a few times. Where are ya? I been by your apartment and called. Nobody has seen ya, and they say you moved out."

Aubrey cleared her throat. "I know, Granny. I'm sorry for not telling you that I was leaving, but I didn't want to worry you. I'm back in town not far from you right now. I was coming to surprise you."

"Oh Lawd, I can't wait 'til you get here. How far are you? Girl, I was so worried 'til I searched for your mama. Neva got her on the phone, tho'. I got to always go through somebody else to get her."

Aubrey was chilled to the bone at the mention of her mother. "What you do that for? She don't give a damn about me. I haven't seen her in over seventeen years. Why would she care now?"

"Now, Bre Bre, don't go getting all worked up. I was desperate, that's all. I reached out to her because she sent you a letter about three weeks ago, and I figured she would be willing to help me find ya. Cut all the fuss out. I will see you in a little bit."

"Yes, ma'am."

Aubrey ended the conversation and headed to her safe haven that she could always count on. She really yearned for the mayhem to stop and for her to finally have a normal life. Her eyes were starting to feel a little better as she rolled her window down to let a little cold air in.

She said aloud, "What letter, and why would my mother be sending me anything after all this time?"

Aubrey sped up, trying to make all the lights that she could. She was about a block away and could see the big country house with the wraparound porch. While tugging at the sewn-in weave, she hoped to take a hot bath and transform back to Aubrey Green and put Martise to rest. As Aubrey pulled up to the house, she could see the light on in the living room. Aubrey parked the car and struggled to take the contacts out of her eyes. She figured she could explain the weave, but the colored contact lenses were overkill; Granny was no fool.

Aubrey looked up to refocus her eyes, and there stood Granny in the door awaiting her arrival. She grabbed her black duffle bag and headed in the house. Aubrey and Granny embraced in the doorway.

Granny held her pretty face in her hands and said, "You are so beautiful, Bre Bre. What you got all that weave in yo' hair fo'?"

Aubrey laughed to take the focus off of her. "Granny, are you gonna let me in, or are we gonna visit in the cold?"

Granny headed in the house, while still going on about Aubrey's hair.

"Granny, I'm twenty-six, and you still treat me like I'm a little girl."

Granny smiled while sliding Aubrey a piece of her favorite pound cake. "Gal, you gonna always be my little girl in pigtails."

Aubrey's face turned to serious, and Granny recognized the shift in her mood.

"Granny, I love you so much, and I thank you for raising me as your own when my mother abandoned me. I swear I will make you proud of me."

Granny wiped away Aubrey's tears. "Gal, what you going on about? You're my own, and I'm proud of you already. You're beautiful and were a big-time manager at the club downtown and all."

Aubrey felt terrible lying to her grandmother for all those years she was actually dancing in the club.

"Well, Granny, you're gonna be even more proud of me. I'm going to be a published author. That's why I left and headed up north."

Granny was so happy that she hugged Aubrey and praised her about her accomplishments. Aubrey took in all the love she had longed for and needed.

Aubrey and Granny were deep into reminiscing, when a faint ringing sound went off four times. They both scanned the room searching for the sound. Aubrey checked her pocket and looked at her phone. They heard the sound again coming from the hallway. Aubrey excused herself, following the sound that led her to the black bag. She opened it and realized it was her spare phone that came with the items from Jimmy. She fumbled as she hit the green button.

"Hello."

"Hey, girl, did I wake you?"

Aubrey cleared her throat. "What time is it?"

"I'm sorry. It's about twelve-thirty. I just got off work, and your letter said if I wanted to see you again, call this number."

"I'm good, Officer Truman. I will miss a little sleep for you." Aubrey laid it, as to make her feel superior.

"I read your letter. That bitch is wicked. How do you deal with her?"

Aubrey remained silent, then hung up. If she were going to get the officer where she wanted her, she would have to be very convincing.

Officer Truman, who sat staring at the receiver, said to herself, "She hung up on me."

Aubrey counted to ten and then dialed the number on her caller ID. The phone rang three times.

"Hello. I had to hang up to be sure this wasn't a set up. As I told you in the letter, Spice is treacherous, and I will not cross her in the light."

Officer Truman took a deep breath. "You're really scared of her, huh? I would never set you up. You told me about her trying to get me a case and fired."

Aubrey said, "How do I know that is real? You could be setting me up for her. Maybe I fell for the wrong officer by..."

Before Aubrey could hang up the phone, Officer Truman yelled, "Wait, Martise! Don't hang up. How could I set you up when I already put a hit out on Spice that will be completed by one-thirty? That's what I was calling to let you know. You don't have to worry about her no more, and you don't have to go to the authorities with her story about me."

Dead silence played in the background like a soundtrack from a scary movie. Aubrey smiled from ear to ear, but kept her act up. Sounds of fake tears surged through the phone.

"Officer Truman, I can't believe you would do that for me. I have to see you tonight. I just have to."

"Girlie, I feel a connection with you, and I'm not like Spice. I protect my woman."

Aubrey gave more fake thank you's as she wrote her address down. "I will be there about two o'clock. I need time to get ready for you, Officer Truman."

"I'll be waiting for you, Martise, and please, call me Gloria. Officer Truman is too formal."

"Okay, Gloria. I will see you soon!"

Aubrey returned to Granny, who had dozed off on the sofa with the television still on. She kissed Granny on the cheek and retired to her old bedroom, but not before starting her bath water so she could get ready for her date with Gloria.

* * * * *

Detective Torrey sat at his desk going over his paperwork from the Jerome and Quanda case. He crossed her name out and wrote the word "murdered" next to it. The once concrete handle that he had on the case was slipping through his fingers rapidly. He reviewed the crime scene pictures and took notes, connecting people to each other and crossing others out. He was not sure how the bodies were connected. Detective Torrey started to believe Spice may not be the killer, or if she was, her charge just went to the next level with three bodies added.

He tapped his pencil on the desk while talking to himself. "This just doesn't add up. The crime was not done by a professional. The crime scene is too random."

Detective Torrey yearned for this case to be solved. He had not slept at home in days. Now with the new bodies, waiting on evidence from the crime lab, and a visit to Spice being needed, he would not see his bed for another couple days.

* * * * *

Aubrey triple checked that she had everything she needed. She quietly left out of the house, closing the door slowly and gently like she had done so many times as a teen when sneaking out. Aubrey hopped in the car trying to escape from the cold air. Starting the ignition, she secured her black bag on the floor in the back.

Aubrey passed light after light. With it being late at night, the streets were free of traffic and pedestrians. A lump formed in her throat when she noticed the bright light from the police helicopter scanning the downtown skyline. She was headed in the opposite direction, but still could not help but feel a sense of anxiousness knowing what she'd done. Aubrey paid close attention to the street signs as not to miss her stop. She was in the Buckhead area of the city. As she made a turn onto Kingsboro Road, she could not believe the luxury in the area. She pulled up to Kingsboro Place Luxury Apartments and headed to apartment D-2.

The grounds of the apartment complex were immaculate. Aubrey could not believe Officer Truman lived in such luxury on her salary. She had to be on the crooked side of corrections.

Aubrey followed her directions from their earlier conversation. She navigated through the entrance procedure with no time to spare. Aubrey prepared her entrance strategy. She stood there with her stylish hat on, black one-piece and right hand in her coat pocket. She called her when she was at the door.

"Hello. I'm at the door."

"Already? You're early. It's only twenty minutes to two. I'm still in the bathroom, but the door is open."

"Okay. I'm coming in."

"Sure. You can join me in the bath, if you'd like, or should I hurry out?"

Aubrey giggled as she played her schoolgirl act. "I'll surprise you."

Aubrey opened the door and was welcomed by a spacious, nicely decorated abode. She cased the apartment while talking long distance to Officer Truman. She needed to be sure that she knew her surroundings just in case things didn't go as planned.

"Where should I put my bag?"

Officer Truman responded, "You can put it in my bedroom. Just follow my voice."

Aubrey made a right turn, passing the laundry room and then the kitchen. She admired the gourmet stove and granite countertops. Aubrey made note of the balcony and second bedroom. She turned right again and entered a spacious master bedroom. A king-sized bed anchored the room with hues of chocolate and tan throughout. Masculine pajamas lay on the bed that could be seen through the flicker of the candlelight. Aubrey continued to entertain her.

"Wow, Gloria! All of this for me? Are you trying to steal my heart?"

Aubrey could hear her moving around in the bathroom. Sounds of the water going down the drain alerted Aubrey that the bath was done.

Officer Truman shouted back, "I wanted you to feel special because you are."

Aubrey took off her coat and hat. She could see Officer Truman through the reflection on the dresser mirror. Officer Truman had her back turned as she gathered her toiletries from around the deep bathtub. Aubrey took her chance and entered the bathroom. Her boots clicked on the tile floor. When Officer Truman stood to an upright position, she found Aubrey directly behind her. Aubrey got extremely close, as if she was a part of her skin, and laid her head on her shoulder while kissing her neck. Officer Truman took a deep breath and turned to see Aubrey's pretty face. She locked eyes with Aubrey's grey piercing stare and dropped all of her belongings. Now out of costume, her black hair fell down her back.

In one motion, Aubrey raised her right hand from her side and pressed a Taser gun into her side, sending high levels of electric currents through Officer Truman's naked body. Her shaking body fell forward into the tub, and she cracked her head on her way down. Aubrey then went to retrieve her tools from her bag and returned to the bathroom to finish the job.

Chapter 13

No Turning Back

The day was off to a good start. Scottie had just finished getting his body pleasured from one of his steady booty calls. The women that he entertained were considered booty calls only because of the no-strings-attached sex contract, but he made it a rule not to get caught up with hungry hoodrats.

He pressed the smartpad on the wall after his guest left. The solar blinds went up, the television came on, and his fireplace ignited in the living room. Wearing nothing but a towel, Scottie stood in front of his massive floor-to-ceiling window taking in the beautiful city view. The Penn Treaty Village Penthouses on Brown Street was where he called home in the city. The entire place was wrapped in clear oversized windows. Stunning waterfront views could be seen anywhere in the condo.

His 51-inch flat-screen television played in the background as he thought about what he had accomplished. In just a few hours, he would be center stage once again at the grand opening of his latest social club, Intoxic. Scottie was happy with his success, but at times like this, he found himself a little lonely with no one to actually share it with. His moment of solitude was interrupted by the ringing from his smartpad alerting him of an incoming call. Scottie pressed a button, and Brooke's voice soared through the surround sound speakers.

"Hey. bighead! Are you ready for tonight?"

"Yes. A soldier is always ready."

Scottie was very happy to hear from Brooke. She always knew when to show up.

"I hear you, but I know this day is bittersweet," she continued. "The more success you acquire, the more you really want your father's approval and recognition of manhood."

Scottie fought back the tears that Brooke's words were fostering. In an attempt to keep his composure, he shot back, "You backyard shrink, I don't need your screwed-up assessment. From my recollection, you got a 'C' in Psychology in college."

The pair shared a laugh. Scottie knew Brooke was on the right track, but he refused to give in to her theory. What she didn't know is that she was the secret object of his desire.

"Brooke, I hope you're ready on time. I know how long you take to get dolled up. So, please, be on time. You've been slipping lately. I'm starting to think you're hiding one of your boy-toys."

With a shaky voice, Brooke quickly chimed in, trying to gather info on what he knew. "Why you say that?"

He laughed at her quick response. "Because you always act weird when you're getting some..."

Brooke became defensive. "Bye, Scottie!"

Recognizing her agitation, he matched it. "Yeah, bye...and don't be late!"

After hanging up the phone, Brooke knew what she had to do.

* * * * *

Aubrey had been back in Philly for a few days. She managed to move into her new place and start the groundwork for her new publishing company. Aubrey sat in the middle of her comfy bed wrapped in her towel. The steam from her hot bath still lingered in the air as it escaped from her master bathroom. She shuffled through the papers that she had lifted from Brea's home office. She had contacts on a flash drive along with a manuscript that Brea was working on the night her life ended. Aubrey had no remorse. She snacked on crackers while reading the contents of the files, planning to get a leg up on LRP.

Her phone rang a few times, but she ignored the calls. Justin's phone calls went from a few times an hour to a few times a day. Aubrey was not giving in, though. She had worked for years doing things that most women would not think of doing to gather her small fortune. Then to add Jerome's large fortune placed her at the top. She was not interested in anyone that did not have millions in the bank. Aubrey had a clear plan, and this time, she was not willing to deviate from it.

Aubrey finished up her research and headed to her walk-in closet to look for something to wear. She had a long day ahead of her: manicure, pedicure, and a full Brazilian waxing. She had to be extra special for her night ahead. Aubrey gathered her Juicy Couture sweat suit and designer tennis shoes, then headed back into the bedroom.

Not paying attention to where she was walking, she stumbled over her black bag and stubbed her toe on the wall. She whined as she bent over to touch her toe. On the floor of her bedroom was the cream-colored envelope that she had taken from her granny. Aubrey really hated her mom and could not imagine what she could have written to her after all the years that melted away. She picked it up and threw it in her bag, making a mental note to read it during her pedicure.

Aubrey did not take long getting ready for her appointment at the spa. With just a few hours to go before show time, she was motivated to hurry. Dressed and standing in the mirror, Aubrey grabbed a fist full of her hair and placed it in a side ponytail. Then she collected her purse and keys and headed out the door.

* * * * *

Brenson was sweating profusely as he struggled to catch his breath. The sound from the treadmill next to him brought him out of his trance. It was about six o'clock on a Saturday evening, and he was running on the treadmill to clear his head. In a few hours, he would be at the Bossin' Up Ball celebrating the boss status of his brother Scottie. The treadmill he was on had reached the end of his forty-five-minute set and was slowing to the cool down phase. His speed went from a sprint to a jog. The red numbers on the touchscreen read 05.00 minutes, and the words cool down scrolled across the screen. A nice workout always helped him clear his mind as well as keep his figure tight.

While admiring a female onlooker, Brenson hopped off the treadmill. He walked by the stretching area where she was warming up before her workout.

"Shit, this is what I'm gonna miss once I snag Brooke exclusively," he whispered to himself through a half smile.

Brenson headed to the free weights to work his muscles out, ending his workout routine with a bang. He sat down and proceeded to do bicep curls one after another. The blue floor mat lay center of the free weight area where two guys challenged each other doing pushups. Brenson did three sets of thirty curls on each arm. By the time he looked up, it was 6:25 p.m. He needed to get home to shower and prepare for his evening, but first, he had to make it to Jewelers Row in Downtown Philly to pick up a couple of items for the evening.

So, he finished up and headed for the locker room. The flirty lady from the stretching area was now on a bike. She waved and winked at Brenson as he walked pass. He returned the favor, disappeared into the men's locker room, and then headed out the back door to his car.

Excitement was in the air, and the city seemed to be buzzing about the opening of the new club. There were Intoxic girls on the streets of Downtown Philly passing out flyers and welcoming all those who wanted to come help celebrate Scottie's new venture. The girls were beautiful and half-dressed, which made for a spectacle. Men stopped and grabbed flyers, and those that couldn't stop honked their horns. Kitty, one of the Intoxic girls, held up a sign that read, Honk if you will be at Intoxic Waterfront Club tonight. Men and women of all walks of life honked their horns, excited that there would be a new upscale club where they could socialize and unwind.

Scottie was good at finding a way to merge cultures and get people to see the one thing they had in common: wanting to live a good life and have a good time. Set in an affluent area right on the waterfront, the club was sure to be a hit. The tickets carried a hefty price tag, and no expense would be spared. Scottie made sure all of his celebrity clients had received special invitations. They would be set up in the five VIP sections that overlooked the main entertainment area.

Kitty stepped in the street when the light turned red and approached the heavily tinted black BMW. She sashayed past the back door on the driver's side of the car. Kitty's legs were shaking from the cold air, but she turned the shaking into a sexy wiggle. As she approached the driver's window, it lowered before she could tap on it. Brenson flashed his pretty smile and winked as he took the flyer. The light changed and he pulled off.

While heading to his jeweler, Brenson smiled at the lengths Scottie went to in order to bring in business for the new social club. Scottie's ability to cross boundaries and look good doing it is what Brenson despised.

When Brenson saw the large diamond ring sign hanging from the top corner of the brick storefront, he knew he had arrived at his destination.

* * * * *

Justin stood behind the desk at the Ritz Carlton wearing a fresh pressed shirt and tie, looking professional as usual. The lobby was full of people and a little more lively than usual on this Saturday night. Weddings and private parties usually filled the hotel with people. However, this night, the Ritz had a more hip crowd in the mix. Justin observed women in crowds of four and dressed in designer clothes floating through the lobby as they headed out the exit. He caught eyes with a particular group and asked the women where they were headed. A tall, light-skinned woman flirted with him by leaning over the front desk and handing him a flyer.

She playfully remarked, "I hope to see you there when you get off, sexy."

Justin smiled as he walked away and headed to help a worker in need. He waited on a couple who were checking in for their pre-honeymoon suite. Looking at the happy couple made Justin feel worse than he already did, but he maintained his composure as he assisted the trainee with the check-in.

As he handed the keys to the groom, he told the happy couple, "Thank you for choosing The Ritz Carlton. Enjoy your stay." He then excused himself and headed to his office.

As he walked down the hallway, he reminisced about the good times he and Aubrey had shared. Justin had been a wreck since Aubrey stormed off under false pretenses and had been refusing his calls. Justin walked and dialed Aubrey's number, hoping for a different response. The phone rang a few times, and then, as usual, her voicemail answered. Justin started to leave a message, but changed his mind as a feeling of sadness set in.

* * * * *

The moment had finally come. Club Intoxic doors would be open for business in a few short minutes. As Scottie approached the well-lit real-estate beauty, the line was down the block. Cars pulled up and were quickly removed by the valet parking attendants. The driver of the limo stopped and jumped out to open Scottie's door. Scottie arrived a little early, and as always, his anxiety was at its highest before revealing another one of his social masterpieces.

The last touches were put on the massive party room, and he was proud of his accomplishment. Scottie walked through each room to be sure all areas of his latest venture were flawless. Scottie gave dap to each security guard as he walked past their area. His place was so upscale that even the security guards wore suits with the hands-free walkie-talkies in their ears, looking like Secret Service men.

After his stamp of approval, he retreated to his office to await his guest. He would be making a grand entrance once the party was underway. Scottie closed the door behind him and headed for his desk to tie up some loose ends for his next business venture.

Fifteen minutes had gone by, and Scottie was finishing up his phone call. The ten-foot gold doors of the club opened, and the celebrators poured in, but not before checking in at the registration tables. Ooo's and ahhh's could be heard throughout the building. Each room was better than the one before. Guests browsed the grounds in their expensive party attire while taking in the panoramic views. Music played throughout the space as people danced and consumed champagne among other spirits. The custom-made bar was positioned in the center of the main party room. Italian marble and mahogany wood played perfectly together, and the seamless lines met at the massive wraparound bar.

The partygoers were from all walks of life, and Scottie had something for everyone. Although the party was flowing in the main party room, he had mini hideaways for sub parties. The younger crowd gravitated to the media lounge, where the mirrored walls were the home of touchscreen computers connected to Facebook and other popular social media sites. The computers allowed his patrons to check-in at Club Intoxic and take pictures that could be automatically uploaded to their profiles.

Scottie enjoyed seeing the party go so well. He could see special guests arriving and being escorted to the various VIP lounges. About thirty minutes into the celebration, Brooke arrived and then Brenson. That was Scottie's cue to make his grand entrance and address his guests. Scottie stood to his feet while talking into his walkie-talkie, giving the signal for the DJ to switch the vibe up and announce him. Before exiting his office, he stopped in front of the mirror and smiled at his reflection as he prepared to greet his guests.

The music in the entire club changed up, and everyone began looking around to see what was going on. The DJ announced Scottie, and all eyes were directed to the spotlight on the balcony that hovered over the main dance floor.

Aubrey had completed all of her most important beauty rituals. She was late, but not too late for her outing. As she sashayed into the main party room, her breath was stolen, leaving her gasping for air. The room was gorgeous. She fell in love with the enormous bar that was obviously the centerpiece of the space. Mahogany columns framed the room, and the marble floor with mahogany inlay for the dance floor was breathtaking. Drink waiters whisked about, keeping the guests' hands filled with champagne.

Aubrey's eyes scanned the room trying to take it all in. She reached out and took a glass of champagne from the waiter's tray. Still looking at what her two hundred dollars had paid for, she spotted a beautiful twenty-foot table that started in the left corner of the room and hugged the walls in a winding fashion. The table was landscaped with colossal shrimp, crudité, fruit, and various exotic hors d'oeuvre.

As Aubrey stood with her back to the crowd in her one-of-a-kind black lace cocktail dress taking in the massive food selection, a smooth deep voice came over the sound system and lingered in the air. The words jarred her from out of her trance and held her captive. Aubrey turned to see the man behind the voice, and there stood Scottie looking down at the crowd. Aubrey became weak in the knees. He was a work of art and looked very different from their first encounter. The money definitely had an advantage, and she was determined to get in his presence one more time.

"Welcome to Club Intoxic, where the luxury is intoxicating! I want to thank all of you who came out tonight to help us celebrate our grand opening of yet another SB brand club. I have to thank my team, who helps the day-to-day operations of SB brand run smoothly."

The crowd cheered loudly. With champagne in hand, Scottie continued as a second spotlight focused on a blushing Brooke. "My partner and right-hand woman Brooke, I would not be here without all of your hard work and belief in my vision years ago. So, to that, I say hold your glasses up, everyone, and join me in a toast."

Everyone followed his directions as he yelled, "Salute!"

The entire club returned the greeting and glasses turned bottoms up all over the club. Then music returned to full blast throughout the space.

Aubrey was on the hunt for a way to get to Scottie before the night was over. She mingled and smiled as she made it through the crowd. Aubrey located the stairs that led up to the second level. Some of the guests lingered on the stairs talking and socializing. Men were in awe of her beauty. Her grey eyes with speckles of green were her main weapon of persuasion.

Aubrey reached the second floor and headed toward the end on the balcony where Scottie stood just moments prior. She came upon a dead end. A decorated wall was all that could be seen. Aubrey was perplexed. From the first level, a room could be seen with an oversized window that sat over the dance floor, but while on the second level, there was no access to that room or area of the club. Frustrated and confused, Aubrey turned and headed back down the hall toward the stairs. When she looked over the balcony, she spotted Scottie standing at the bar sharing a laugh with Brooke. Aubrey hurried down the stairs, trying not to lose him again. The women were on the prowl, and she had no intentions of being beat out by a bunch of groupies.

Brooke and Scottie embraced and share some laughs. Brooke was so proud of her friend, and she let him know it as she leaned in to whisper in his ear. Brenson, who was positioned on the balcony, watched in disgust as Scottie and Brooke flirted back and forth. He hated that Scottie really could have Brooke if he wanted. Brenson was confident in the fact that Scottie feared ruining their relationship, so he would not try to seduce Brooke. Brenson clinched his glass in his hand tightly the closer Brooke and Scottie got. He was pissed off that he did not get mentioned by name in Scottie's speech. Brenson had to think quickly and put his plan in motion. He knew it was time to execute it.

Brenson took his phone out of his pocket and dialed the number. Then he watched as Brooke reached inside her small evening bag to retrieve her cell phone.

Across the room, Aubrey was moving at a brisk steady pace, trying to make it to Scottie before he disappeared into the crowd. She walked fast while trying not to fall in her six-inch heels. Aubrey noticed Brooke whisper something in Scottie's ear before she turned to walk away.

Brooke and Aubrey caught eyes, and Brooke looked as if she had seen a ghost. Aubrey waved at Brooke while getting closer. Brooke waved back and hurried off in the opposite direction, thinking that Aubrey was headed for her. She quickly took the long way around to the stairs as she looked back to see if Aubrey had followed her.

Aubrey was inches away from the bar and noticed that Scottie was finishing up his drink when three groupies approached him, asking to take pictures with him. Annoyed at first, Aubrey turned up her nose at the desperate trio. However, she soon appreciated the role that the trio served. She finally reached the bar and was able to position herself in close proximity to Scottie. As Scottie got acquainted with the girls, Aubrey posted up at the bar, opting not to take a seat. She stood in a perfect position as if posing for a photo shoot, with drink in hand and her curvaceous silhouette on display.

Just as she planned, Scottie turned around and she was in his view.

Scottie gestured for the bartender to give him another one of his favorites: Ciroc straight up with a lemon on the side. He tossed back his beverage and then bit on the lemon. He immediately noticed Aubrey. She was like a red spot in an all-white room. She stood out in any setting. He looked at her closely from head to toe. Her long, curly tresses had been pressed out and hung past her mid-back. Aubrey could see Scottie staring at her out of her peripheral vision. She enjoyed the attention and knew she had to go all out if she wanted to land him.

Aubrey leaned in toward the male bartender, and with the words escaping her full, red lips, she seductively said, "I will have a dirty martini."

Aubrey timed her stare perfectly. While tossing her hair over her right shoulder, she looked up and their eyes locked. Only a few feet away, Scottie held his glass up and smiled at her. Aubrey flashed a seductive grin in response. Then it hit Scottie where he had seen her before. He could never forget her alluring eyes and exotic skin tone.

Scottie approached Aubrey. "Hello, beautiful lady. I guess you decided to allow me to show you my city after all."

Aubrey giggled and put on the fakest memory loss act that she could. "Excuse me?"

Scottie gave her a look again. "You are new in town, right?"

Aubrey tossed her hair again and replied, "Yes. How did you know that?"

Now feeling the effects of his three shots of Ciroc, Scottie stepped back and opened his suit jacket. "You really don't remember me?"

Aubrey fluttered her eyelashes. "Should I remember you?"

Scottie had a feeling she was taking him for a ride, but he was not backing down. He knew that she remembered him. His vision of Aubrey became a little clearer, and he was willing to test his theory.

"As beautiful as you are, I would never forget that face, but I could be mistaken. Sorry to interrupt your drink." Scottie turned and began to walk away.

Aubrey panicked. She had worked hard to get to him, and in a blink of an eye, she lost him. Scottie made his way through the crowd, waving at familiar faces as he headed toward the private elevator to his office. Aubrey was in tow, and Scottie did not realize it until he felt a hand touch his left shoulder. He turned and she gave him a smile.

"I just remembered where I saw you before." Aubrey walked around Scottie seductively as he followed her with his eyes, smiling all the while.

Scottie replied, "Is that right? I'm listening."

As she leaned against him, she said, "I was fresh off of the train, and you nearly killed me running by."

Scottie stepped away from her and spun around being silly. Holding one side of his jacket open, he replied, "I do clean up nice. No wonder you didn't recognize me."

They shared a laugh as their heavy flirting continued. Aubrey had regained her position and worked to seal the deal. She extended her hand toward Scottie.

"My name is Aubrey. It's nice to formally meet you."

Scottie grabbed her hand and breathed a sigh of relief at how soft they were. He took a moment just to stare in her eyes.

"The name is Scottie. Nice to meet you, as well."

Aubrey giggled. "Shall we return to the bar, or do you have something a little more private in mind?"

Scottie was taken back at Aubrey's candor. He gestured toward the bar, and the pair returned to the bar where two seats were ready for their arrival.

As Aubrey sat at the bar laying the foundation for the next level of her plan, Brooke was upstairs receiving what felt like the shock of her life. Brooke followed Brenson's instructions to the letter once she received his phone call. In her eyes, Brenson had been missing in action all evening, and she found that a little odd. Brooke followed the well-lit hallway toward the sky room. She saw guests exiting the room as she came closer to the lounge. Brooke checked her watch as the night was winding down. She was curious as to Brenson's plans. She hated being alone with Brenson whenever Scottie was around. Brooke feared Scottie would figure out that she and Brenson were doing the naked tango.

Brooke entered the room to find Brenson staring out of the window. The beautifully styled room gave the impression that one was sitting in the sky. The clear glass wall touched the floor, creating the illusion that the floor disappeared off the edge of the building. Brenson heard Brooke's heels against the marble floor, and he turned to greet her.

"Hey, beautiful. You are the sexiest woman in the building."

Brooke smiled. "Hey, Bren. I've been looking for you ever since I arrived here."

Brenson knew that was a lie, but continued anyway. Reaching out, he pulled Brooke close to him and kissed her lips. Brooke gently retracted.

"Bren, what are you doing? Not here."

Brenson spun her around playfully. "Why not? It's time that I let the world know how we feel about each other."

Brooke pulled away and walked over to stare at the city view. She had been struggling to break it off with Brenson for days and just couldn't do it, especially after the night at his place. Brenson approached her from behind and put his arms around her waist. Brooke's body tensed.

"Bren, we need to talk."

Brenson squeezed her tight and kissed her neck. In between smooches, he spoke. "Brooke, we do need to talk, but let me go first." He got close to her ear as they looked at the

Philadelphia view of the city. Brenson took a deep breath then continued. "I was not expecting us to fit so perfectly. I am totally in love with you. I cannot imagine us keeping this a secret any longer."

Brooke's body tensed even more, until she finally turned to face him. Brenson let the words go when he saw her face.

"Will you marry me?"

Brooke's face said many things, but love was not one of them. There stood Brenson in an Armani suit, holding a five-carat classic solitaire diamond set in a twisted platinum band. Brooke was speechless. She had imagined this moment all of her life. The atmosphere was perfect, and the backdrop was flawless. But, the key player was all wrong. Brooke finally mustered up the words.

"Brenson, I'm sorry. I never knew you were so serious about us." Tears began to flow from Brooke's eyes. "I can't. I just can't. What would Scottie say?"

Brenson stood there watching his master plan crumble before him. He was so sure that Brooke was falling for him. For the first time, he was faced with the truth about why Brooke agreed to keep their relationship a secret. She was just as in love with Scottie as he was with her. Scottie had beaten him for the last time.

Downstairs in the party, Scottie and Aubrey were enjoying one another's company so much that he never saw Brenson storm out with Brooke following behind him. Aubrey pulled out all the stops. She was charming and polite, with a twist of sexy. There was plenty of alcohol involved, and she was throwing them back. Feeling the chemistry between them and the itch in his groin, Scottie leaned in to speak to Aubrey.

"Hey, do you still want to get a little more private? I can have my car come around to get us."

Knowing she only had one shot to put it on him and have him begging for more, she said, "Sure. I would like to be able to talk to you without having to yell." Her statement was safe, but true.

Scottie attempted to stand to his feet, but swayed from side to side. He gestured for the security guy at the front door to call his car. Aubrey followed him through the club in the opposite direction of the front entrance. They continued to make small talk while walking side by side. Finally, they made it through the club and came upon a door that led to a private parking lot. The sky was clear, and the stars twinkled a little brighter. Their warm breath was visible as it competed with the cold air.

As the limo pulled up in front of them, Scottie grabbed her hand and said, "Ladies first always."

She obliged and entered the limo. Soon, Scottie was inside, and their transportation whisked them off to their destination.

* * * * *

Brooke followed Brenson, trying to finish their necessary discussion. She felt so bad that she had sexed him and dated him for a good while with no intentions on moving forward. She never meant for anyone's feelings to get hurt.

Brenson drove through the streets of Philadelphia with his windows down and music blasting. His driving was reckless. He disregarded traffic lights and beeped for people to get out of the street. Brooke followed him, trying to catch up with him before he had an accident. She hit speed dial on her phone, but Brenson's voicemail came on every time. He sped down Delaware Avenue with Brooke on his tail. Brooke was ready to call Scottie, when she noticed Brenson's car slowing down. After he pulled into an empty pier lot, Brooke slowly approached his vehicle. She found Brenson humped over the steering wheel of his car chanting something under his breath over and over. Brooke called his name.

"Brenson, come on. We need to talk. Please, just calm down and talk to me."

Brenson turned slowly to look at her and then began to laugh hysterically. Clinching the steering wheel, he started at Brooke. "Bitch, please. Talk about what? You used me as your little boy toy, all the while pining after the great Scottie! I was good enough to give you those multiple orgasm that you love so much, but when I present you with a flawless diamond, all bets are off. Fuck you! We have nothing to talk about."

Brooke stood there with her mouth open so wide that her tongue hung out of it. She stepped back from the car, almost as if she were making sure she had heard Brenson correctly.

"Brenson, is this how you behave, like a child? You're angry. I get that. But, there's no need to be insulting. I..."

Brenson cut her off. "Hold it right there, high and mighty Brooke. You don't get the chance to give a fucking speech. I fucked you, sucked you, wined and dined you. You even told me how great I was, but you could never see yourself marrying me. Or should I say you see yourself marrying Scottie, huh?"

He took a deep breath as Brooke started to retreat to her car, but Brenson was not done. He got out of his car and yelled some more.

"Yeah, that's right. I know your sick secret. You want Scottie. But, guess what? You will never have him once I give him the play-by-play details of our sexfest. That's what it was, right? See you at work, you heartless bitch!"

Brenson knew deep down inside that if he told Scottie of their affair, he ran the risk of him cutting him off too soon. However, the rage and hatred that he felt toward Brooke seemed worth it.

Brooke hopped in her car and pulled out of the parking lot in reverse. Trying to keep her sight clear, she wiped her eyes as her mascara ran. As she headed home, Brooke searched her front seat for her cell phone. She came to a red light and had to slam on the brakes. Finally, she located her phone and hit the number one on speed dial.

* * * * *

Scottie scanned his key, and the front door opened. He escorted Aubrey inside and welcomed her to make herself comfortable. As Aubrey canvassed the place, she saw nothing but style and luxury throughout the space. Scottie touched his smartpad on the wall next to the front door. The curtains opened, fireplace lit up, and music started to play all at once. Although impressed, she did not want to appear too eager.

"Scottie, you have a beautiful home. I love the detailed woodwork around your molding," she commented.

He gave Aubrey a point for noticing something so detailed. While gathering wine glasses and wine from his wine cooler, he talked to her from a distance. "Thanks. I do love my place. I'm glad you like it, too."

By the time Scottie returned to the living room, Aubrey had taken off her shoes and her pocketbook lay on the coffee table. She took a glass out of his hand and held it up as if to ask him to pour the wine. Scottie poured the chardonnay, filling the glass halfway. Then he poured his own. They both sipped, and then Aubrey finished her glass off.

Scottie sat back on the sofa and placed his hand on her inner thigh. Feeling tingles in places she longed for, Aubrey decided to skip the teenage make-out session. She mounted Scottie and kissed him passionately, then pulled back and looked into his eyes. Scottie stared back in a masculine but sexy manner. He slid both hands up her thighs and proceeded north until he could feel her soft breasts in his hands. Going in for the kill, he unzipped her dress while licking on her neck. Just then, Scottie felt a vibration in his pants. He looked at Aubrey strangely, and they both looked down. He felt it again.

They both laughed as Aubrey, who was now half naked, leaned to the side to allow him to reach into his pocket. Scottie retrieved his phone and hit the button to answer the call.

Breathing heavily, he said, "Hello!"

Aubrey continued to kiss his neck and now her hand was in his drawers massaging his manhood.

"Hello, Scottie. Are you busy? I wanted to come over."

Scottie could not hear the concern in her voice over the heavy breathing and moaning Aubrey was doing.

"Brooke, sorry, but not to night," he replied. "You have the worse timing. We can celebrate another night." Grabbing Aubrey's breast out of her bra, he continued. "I'm kind of into something right now."

He did not even give Brooke enough time to respond. Scottie hung up the phone and threw it across the room.

Aubrey continued to undress Scottie, exposing his rock-hard abs. For Aubrey, looks usually wasn't the turn on, but in Scottie's case, he had looks and money, which made it a lot easier. Aubrey stood in front of him, exposing every inch of her beautiful frame. Scottie was fully erect as he fantasized about what he was going to do to her.

Aubrey walked from one end of the sofa to the other, as if being showed off at a brothel. She stopped in front of him, turned to face her round ass toward him, and then sat straight back, allowing her wet cave to swallow every inch of him. Scottie moaned with excitement as Aubrey's bottom smacked his lap and wiggled with each stroke.

Chapter 14
Glass Ceiling

The body count in Atlanta had just gone up and was connected to what Detective Torrey thought was a crime of passion. His theory had quickly changed, and he was headed to the prison to visit with Spice, hoping if she was in connection with the crimes that she would be willing to talk.

Detective Torrey arrived at the county jail where Spice was being held. Approaching the front desk, he proceeded to push past the masses that filled the lobby. He overheard two females complaining about how long the wait had been for visitation. He finally made it past the crying babies and frustrated female visitors who were half dressed and being turned away. He feared he would be stuck waiting in line with the rest of the visitors, until he saw a beacon of hope, which came in the form of a short, heavyset man wearing a lieutenant's uniform and hat. Detective Torrey approached the white shirt to ask if he could bypass the red tape.

Detective Torrey got closer, and while standing behind him, he said, "Excuse me, sir."

Seeming annoyed, the lieutenant turned toward him, but never looked up from his clipboard. "Yes, how may I help you?"

Detective Torrey cleared his throat as to encourage the lieutenant to at least look up at him. The lieutenant finally lifted his head, wanting to see the person who was being extremely annoying. When the men met eyes, they both smiled and embraced. They knew each other from college.

"Hello, Torrey. What are you doing in these parts?"

"This is my home now, Ernie. I'm a detective down here. That's actually why I'm here today."

"Okay, big guy. Let me get you checked in so you don't lose your place, and then we can talk."

The lieutenant told one of his officers to check Detective Torrey in. Doing as told, the officer took all of his information and checked his ID and badge.

Lieutenant Ernie stepped up and asked, "Torrey, who are you here to see? I want to get them prepared for visitation."

Looking at his friend, Detective Torrey replied, "Cindy Dorsey. I have some turns in the case and want to press her to see if she'll answer some more questions."

The lieutenant and the officer at the front desk looked at each other. Lieutenant Ernie pulled Detective Torrey aside and told him to follow him.

"You need to speak with the warden. I hate to inform you of this, but your primary suspect is dead. She was found in the laundry room this morning with a sheet wrapped around her neck and stuffed in a laundry basket with the sheets."

Detective Torrey's eyes grew wide; he shifted his weight on each foot back and forth.

"What? This can't be happening." As Detective Torrey followed the lieutenant to the warden's office, he knew he was in for a long day.

* * * * *

Aubrey awoke to the smell of strong coffee. She could hear the pots in the kitchen being placed on the stove. Aubrey arched her back, climbed out of bed, and prepared to head to the kitchen to greet Scottie in the nude. She bent over to shake out her long hair, which had turned curly from their midnight bedroom romp fest. She tiptoed, hoping her actions would be looked at as cute and playful, not desperate. She turned the corner and entered the kitchen, where she could see the refrigerator open and a food spread for a queen.

"Good morning, sleepyhead."

The refrigerator door closed, and up popped a white man holding a tray of fruit. Aubrey yelled, and the man dropped the tray as he gazed at her nakedness. Scottie came running from the master bathroom wrapped in a towel. He saw Aubrey standing there naked and Chef André apologizing in broken English. Scottie began to laugh as Aubrey ran back to the bedroom. She gathered her belongings and was dressed in a matter of minutes. He followed behind her so he could get dressed and prepare to drive her home. Still embarrassed, Aubrey walked quickly by the kitchen. Scottie giggled as he grabbed some breakfast to go.

The drive home was quiet at first, except for the few times that Aubrey and Scottie giggled about her flashing Chef André. Scottie drove while Aubrey looked out of the window. He tried to ignore her phone going off every few blocks.

By the fifth time, he looked at her and asked, "Pretty girl, you gonna get that? Seems like someone is really trying to reach you."

Aubrey smiled and replied, "Like yours last night? I'm cool. I'm with who I want to be with. I'll call them later."

Scottie smiled and took note that Aubrey was ahead of herself after one night of sex. "Is that right? Well, in that case, let the muthafucka ring."

They both laughed at Scottie's silly faces.

"Yo, Aubrey, I will never forget the look on Chef André's face, and I'm sure he won't forget you."

Aubrey reached over and gave Scottie a love tap. "You're horrible, but I really like you."

Scottie pulled in front of her building and parked. In between laughter, he replied, "I like you, too, Aubrey but you're gonna have to come to breakfast naked every time now. Chef André requested it."

Aubrey giggled. "See you later, Scottie. Thanks for the ride."

Before she got out of the car, Scottie leaned over and kissed her. Aubrey sashayed away, hoping he was staring at her, but Scottie had already pulled off.

Aubrey was so happy to be in her new condo and was enjoying having somewhere that she could actually call home. Upon entering her condo, she removed her shoes. Aubrey walked across her living room floor and spread her toes to get comfortable. She turned on her fireplace to get the condo toasty and then passed the kitchen, heading for her bedroom to prepare her bath. While her water filled the tub, Aubrey traveled back to the kitchen to whip something up for breakfast. She placed a bagel in the toaster and prepared the cream cheese and jelly. Next, she grabbed the coffeemaker and unwrapped it. She read the directions to the fancy coffeepot and started a pot of pure Columbian coffee.

Aubrey almost forgot about her water, and she ran to the back to turn it off. The tub was filled, and Aubrey's breakfast was done. She sat at the island in the center of the kitchen eating her continental breakfast, while thinking about her night with Scottie and her next move toward her goal. As she sipped from her coffee, she quietly celebrated her meeting Scottie and being more than halfway to having it all: a rich man and career that she could be proud of. Aubrey's daydreaming was cut short when her doorbell rang. Not expecting anyone, she immediately prepared for the worse.

"Just a minute!" she yelled as she went to the door with her stun gun in hand.

"Aubrey, it's me," a muffled male voice said from the other side.

She smiled at the thought of Scottie coming back to make a house call. However, when she opened the door, there stood Justin looking wild by his eyes. Aubrey tried to close the door, but Justin put his foot in the doorway to stop the door from closing. Surprised at his aggression, she dropped the stun gun.

"Look, Aubrey, I've been calling you for days. Why are you acting this way? We had something good!"

She could not believe Justin was unraveling at the seams. "Justin, how the hell did you get up here?"

He grew angrier because she dismissed his line of questioning and acted as if they were just casual acquaintances. "Aubrey, I saw you get out of that guy's car. Who the hell is he? Is that why you just cut off all communication with me like I was nothing?" Justin pounded his fist on the wall by her door. "You owe me an explanation. I will not be toyed with."

Justin was now inside of the condo and approaching Aubrey in a rage. Aubrey encouraged Justin to leave.

"Justin, it's over! Just accept it! What do you want from me? We were just..."

Aubrey's words were cut off by Justin's hand wrapping around her neck. Aubrey scratched and winced as she tried to get her footing.

"I'm not a toy to be played with, Aubrey Green!" Justin yelled angrily.

Struggling for air, Aubrey pounded on his chest. Justin realized what he was doing as her hits became slower and weaker. He released his grip, and Aubrey dropped to the floor, where she laid holding her throat and scrambling to reach her stun gun. Justin looked around, and seeing the aftermath of his rage, he hurried towards the door. Aubrey watched as Justin made his escape. After pulling herself together and standing to her feet, she quickly made it to her front door and slammed it shut. As Aubrey went to lock the door, she heard two loud thumps and the door flew open. Startled, she jumped back. She was sure Justin had come back to finish her off. She could not believe her eyes. Her day had just gone from bad to worse quickly.

At the door stood three police officers. The tall man in the middle dressed in plain clothes was clearly the leader. He reached his hand out with a gesture to shake Aubrey's hand.

"Hello, my name is Detective Mathews. Can I have a word with you, Ms. Green?"

Still shaken from Justin's tirade, Aubrey grabbed her throat and massaged it as she spoke. "Sure, detective. What about?"

The detective scanned the immediate area surrounding the door and noticed the stun gun lying on the floor. "We need to talk to you about Brea Tillman, owner of LRP. We are investigating her murder."

The detective, who was trained in reading body language, noticed that Aubrey's eyes twitched and she tensed up when Brea's name was mentioned. This indicated to the detective that she was hiding something.

Keep it together, Aubrey, she told herself. They have nothing.

"What murder? And what does that have to do with me?" she asked him.

Detective Mathews played with his keys in his pocket. "I think it will be best if you put some shoes on and came with us. We can finish our conversation down at the station."

Aubrey resisted. "With all due respect, sir, I have a right to know what I have to do with this mess."

Detective Mathews became annoyed. "Look, Ms. Green, we can do this the easy way, where you go to the station willingly, or the hard way, where these two officers handcuff you and bring you in for questioning. It's up to you."

Aubrey thought quickly. She wanted no more physical aggression for the day, so she decided to take the easy way. Still dressed from the night before, she retrieved her Marco flats and headed out the door.

* * * * *

Scottie called Brooke's phone several times, but did not get an answer. He wanted to get together with her to talk about the success of the grand opening and plan his next venture at the club.

Scottie pulled up in front of Liberty Place Mall. He was in need of some basic items and decided to take advantage of his location. He parked the car and got out to feed the meter. He double checked the locks on his Jaguar before entering the mall. Scottie knew he was in center city, but he did not trust people anywhere. Entering the mall, he decided to conduct a little business to lay out his next club takeover. As he dialed the phone, he had an incoming call. He out his dialing short and answered the call.

"Hello," Scottie said as he walked through the mall.

"I have something you have to hear."

Captivated by the caller, Scottie found a bench in the mall and sat down.

* * * * *

Detective Torrey arrived back at his desk. He needed to call an emergency meeting with his captain. Detective Torrey had just been handed a shitload of information and was no closer to solving the murder case that now had a body count of five bodies, all of which were somehow connected to the case.

Detective Torrey sat down and rested his head in the palm of his hands. He was exhausted, and the case seemed to be growing in hard work. He shuffled through the items on his desk, looking for the file he had on Spice, Quanda, and Jerome. Sipping his coffee, he used his left hand to move papers around. Upon noticing an unopened envelope with his name on it, his eyes lit up with excitement. Detective Torrey opened the envelope and began to read its contents.

The DNA results from the hospital test were checked against their stored criminal DNA. The swabs taken from Quanda's mouth matched the DNA from the fluid found on the sheets. Detective Torrey became more excited as he continued to read the report. He was now at the bottom of page one. He sat back in his seat and began to speculate about what went on at Jerome's place that night.

When Detective Torrey turned the page, what he saw changed the whole momentum of his investigation. The results were clear. Cindy Dorsey's (Spice) DNA did not match any of the fluids found at the scene. Moreover, her fingerprints were only on the handle of the front door. Detective Torrey felt like crap. Not only was Spice probably innocent, but also, she was dead because she had been placed in jail.

He took another sip of his coffee and then a bite of his Danish. The next section of the report talked about the DNA correlations that were found. His back stiffened, and he sat up on the edge of his seat. The noisy precinct turned into background noise, and he was totally focused. DNA from female subject A was found on sheets and connected to DNA inside of victim 1's mouth and fingernails as well as on victim 2's right hand. Detective Torrey knew he had a totally different crime scene than he originally suspected. The report was conclusive as it outlined the possibilities in crime theories.

He read on as the report came to a close. In bold letters, the report read DNA for female subject A, NO MATCH FOUND. It was as if the breath had been snatched out of Detective Torrey's lungs. The fact were clear the new suspect was female and not in the system. He felt hopeless. His possible killer had no priors, so the DNA was useless. He was just about to call it quits, when he read further down on the paper. The section looked like instructions or general crime lab information. He looked closely, and it read, A familial DNA search is a search by law enforcement in DNA databases for genetics ... of the relatives of those whose DNA has been collected through the penal system results below. Right below the explanation were two partial matches of family members for the unknown female's DNA. The names were familiar, but he had to do some research to connect the dots.

* * * * *

Aubrey sat in a hard metal chair at a wooden table located in a dimly lit room. Across the table were Detective Mathews and a female Spanish-speaking detective. Aubrey had been in the interrogation room for so long that she had lost track of time. Detective Mathews had been questioning Aubrey for hours. He would take a break, and his partner Detective Perez would jump in. Aubrey purposely kept her mouth shut, choosing only to answer questions that had no real substance. The problem was Aubrey felt as if she was justified to murder Brea, so she was not budging.

Detective Mathews had enough; he was sick of playing it safe with Aubrey. Towering over her, he said, "So, Ms. Green, are you are sure you don't want your call now? Because you're going to be here for a long time."

Aubrey continued to play his game, acting scared and confused as if the detectives were in control. She looked at Detective Mathews and gave him the "deer caught in headlights" look.

"I have no one to call, sir. I still don't understand why I'm here, but I will cooperate fully because I have nothing to hide."

Able to smell when a woman used her charm from a mile away, the female detective became agitated. She always joked that men were the stupidest things ever created. She got all in Aubrey's face, close enough that their noses touched.

"Look, little missy, your innocent act does not cut it with me! We know you had a heated argument with Brea, and you were in a rage because she insulted your work. I've seen people kill for less. Her partner described your behavior at the business meeting as psychotic. Now, all of a sudden, you are Miss Polite Pearl from the south."

Becoming annoyed, Aubrey removed her hands off of the table and began digging her nails into her legs under the table. She obviously had a problem with women, and it was beginning to show. Detective Mathews noticed the change in her eyes. It was the first sign of emotion that she let show in the almost eight hours she had been in interrogation.

Detective Perez walked away from Aubrey and paced the floor as she continued to talk. "We know you're hiding something, and we will find out, chica. We will find out."

Seeing that Perez was able to affect her, Detective Mathew felt they were on to something. As he approached the door, he said, "I'm gonna leave you two together. You seem to have a lot to talk about."

Mathews then exited the room, leaving Aubrey and Perez alone.

Perez turned and smiled at Aubrey. "Finally, all alone."

Aubrey stared at her with hatred, while Perez continued.

"Now where was I, chica? Oh yeah, I was telling your slick ass that I know you did it, and when I find that little piece of evidence that I need...well, let's just say I'm gonna nail your cute ass to the wall!"

Aubrey continued to stare at her. If looks could kill, Perez would have been taking a dirt nap. Perez could tell she was getting to her, so she continued to poke her.

"You're weak! I bet you thought you were so big when Brea begged you to let her live, huh? Well, I have a newsflash for you. A real bitch would have killed her and faced the consequences, not run like a little bitch." Perez slammed her fist on the table.

Aubrey began to laugh as she continued to dig her nails in her thighs. Perez became more annoyed, her adrenaline pumping while sitting across from Aubrey as she watched her throw her head back in laughter.

Perez got up and continued talking as she walked toward the door. "I'm glad you find this amusing. Let's see how funny this is when Mr. Tillman shows up to pick you out of a lineup."

Aubrey stood to her feet and yelled, "I want to call my lawyer!"

Perez turned to face Aubrey and started walking closer to her, then firmly placed her hand on her shoulder while pushing down.

"Sit your ass down. Don't get confused about who you're fucking with, chica."

Aubrey pulled away, but Perez kept on. She leaned close to Aubrey's face until they were cheek to cheek.

Perez spoke softly. "By the way, I read the story you submitted to LRP, and I agree with Brea. Sassy was weak, just like you."

Aubrey pushed away from the table while yelling, "Fuck you! Fuck you! I'll show you weak!"

Just then, Detective Mathews busted through the door, shouting, "Sit down, Ms. Green! Now! Perez, please leave."

Aubrey sat down, but continued to speak as she tried to gain her composure. "Detective Mathews, I asked for my lawyer. I will not be speaking until my lawyer is present, and I need my one phone call, too."

Detective Mathews excused himself from the interrogation room, while Aubrey awaited her requests to be granted. She sat at the table all alone, rocking as she attempted to get Detective Perez's words out of her mind. She mumbled and hummed to herself.

The next time the door to the interrogation room opened up, a medium-build white man entered the room and began to speak. "Ms. Aubrey Green?"

Aubrey looked up at him and responded, "Yes."

He continued. "You are free to go."

Aubrey replied, "What? You mean to tell me I'm not being retained?"

The officer dressed in a regular uniform shook his head as he held the door open. "No, you were just in for questioning. You are free to go."

Aubrey stood up and headed out of the door with hatred in her veins and revenge in her heart.

She stormed out of the police station looking for a ride back to her place. She walked a few blocks over to 12th and Filbert Street. Now dark and cold, she ran the risk of getting lost. Aubrey took her phone out of her purse and prepared to find a ride. When she powered it on, she saw she had about ten missed calls. Many of them were from Justin, and about three recent missed calls were from her granny. She was surprised her granny had called so many times, especially being as though she had just spoken to her the day before. Aubrey logged into her voicemail, skipping all of Justin's voicemails until she came to the messages from her granny.

"Baby, call ya granny. I really need to talk to you." Aubrey skipped to the next one. "Aubrey, I hope you're okay. Please, just call and talk to me." The message was left a few hours later.

Aubrey looked at the phone. Something in her voice was not right. She erased the two messages and played the last message, which was time stamped less than an hour prior.

"Aubrey, I'm really worried about you, baby. You can talk to me. I will explain everything. Please call me."

Now concerned about the phone calls, Aubrey tried to figure out what her granny could have possibly been referring to. She saved the message, planning to listen to it again later.

"I don't have time for this shit, granny," Aubrey said out loud. "I have a lot to handle."

Although she was perplexed by her current situation, she continued to think about her granny's messages. She looked through her purse to find Scottie's card that he gave her. She needed a friend in the worse way, and he was just what the doctor ordered. Aubrey dialed his number and waited for him to pick up. She was directed to his voicemail all three times when she called him. On the third call, she decided to leave a message.

"Hello, Scottie. I hate to bother you, but I'm kind of lost without my car and need to take you up on your offer to be my tour guide. Please call me." Aubrey looked up at the street signs to be sure she provided him with the correct location.

"I'm on the corner of 12th and Filbert. If you can't call, just come."

Aubrey hung up and closed her jacket tighter to keep warm as she waited for Scottie's call. While standing there, she hoped he showed up. Then she thought about her granny's message again. Aubrey got the feeling the letter from her mother may have something to do with her message. She made a note to read it when she reached home.

Chapter 15
By Any Means

Brooke awoke in a bad mood. She was not feeling her best emotionally, and her body seemed to be breaking down, as well. As Brooke rolled over and searched her nightstand for her alarm clock, she managed to knock everything over. She sat straight up, now annoyed with the fact that she had to get out of bed to not only cut off the buzzer, but to clean up the contents from the nightstand off of the floor.

She decided to take a steam shower, hoping it would help her sinuses. Still shaky from her slumber, she walked to the bathroom, but not before turning on the early news to catch the weather and check to see how much traffic she would have to fight through.

Brooke entered her luxurious bathroom. As she spread her toes on the large, plush bath rug, she continued her quest and turned the shower on. She watched the steam fill the room as she used the toilet. Brooke had not spoken to Scottie except briefly two days after the party. Since the night of the party, her conscience had been killing her about Brenson, and to find out that Scottie went home with Aubrey haunted her even more. She was worried Brenson had got to him first and he was upset about what he had been told. Brooke washed her hands as she planned to end the suspicion for good.

* * * * *

Aubrey lay in her soaker tub surrounded by candles. A few days had gone by since she had to walk in the bitter cold to find a cab, and she still had not gotten a call from Scottie. She cozied up in the tub with her pen and pad, adding finishing touches to her newest story. Aubrey had to destroy the items she had taken took from Brea's home office. Detective Mathews and Perez made it clear they would keep fighting to nail her on Brea's murder.

Really wanting things to work out with Scottie, Aubrey tried to rethink her strategy. She placed her pen and pad on the floor by the tub and lay back as she got lost in her thoughts. She began to drift off to sleep as her body relaxed even more in the warm water. Aubrey felt her body slipping away, and she sat straight up, startled by the warm water touching her lips. A shaken Aubrey got out of the bath as not to drown herself. She released the water from her tub and walked through her massive bathroom naked as she towel dried her hair.

Aubrey entered her closet to retrieve something to wear. On the way to the closet, she turned the radio on to listen to the Steve Harvey Morning Show. She'd had a rough few days and needed to laugh about other people's problems. Aubrey's closet was professionally organized when she first moved in her place. However, it had quickly become disorganized from her searching for outfits daily. She needed to call her housekeeping service for a touch up.

To her, it felt like "jeans and a cute t-shirt" kind of day. She turned left at the dresses and there her extensive designer jean collection hung.

"Awww, my babies, which one of you will I wear today?" she said aloud.

Aubrey moved around jeans until she came to her favorite pair of hip-hugging denim. She reached up and pulled her navy blazer from the shelf. She then looked through her shirts hanging and opted to go with a heather grey v-neck and multi-color scarf.

When Aubrey turned to exit her closet, she tripped over her black Kenneth Cole messenger bag. She stumbled a few feet and grabbed on to the wall as her clothing went flying. Breathing rapidly from the scare of almost falling, Aubrey bent down to retrieve her clothes from the floor. As she bent over, there it sat halfway out of the purse. She had misplaced the letter her granny had given her. After Aubrey received the messages from her granny a few days prior, she had searched high and low, but could not find the letter. She thought it was lost forever. She gathered her clothes and the letter, then headed to her bedroom to find out what the big fuss was all about before she talked to her granny next.

Aubrey laid her stylish outfit on the arm of her comfy recliner that sat next to her bed. Wrapped in a towel, she climbed to the center of her king-sized bed and prepared herself for the next chapter in her life. Aubrey opened the letter and took a deep breath before reading the first line. As she read, tears flowed down her face, not really because of its contents, but because of the emotion attached to the first correspondence from her mother in sixteen years.

Dear Bre-Bre,

I don't even know if I can still call you that. If this letter reaches you, I pray you can understand what I am telling you. I know I have not been the best mother, but you would not believe what I had to go through since I left Atlanta. I am not looking for sympathy, but I want you to know I have thought of you often since the day I left. If you don't know by now, hopefully you will find out the truth one day. For now, I am writing to warn you about danger that may befall you. I hate to give you this news by mail, but I have no choice. I am risking my life by writing this. You have a half-sister name Savahnge, and she is not a good person. She is out to get me and anything that I am connected to. I never told her about you, but I have reason to believe she found out about you recently. A few weeks ago, I received an envelope that contained a picture that looks like you. I have not seen you in a while, but I know your eyes anywhere. She is dangerous. If you come in contact with her, please call the authorities. This is the only time I will write you...

Aubrey felt sick to her stomach. She cried harder than she even knew she could. It was the first letter she had received from her mom since sixteen years ago, and she had to learn about a half-sister because she's crazy.

"How could you leave me and go have another daughter?" Aubrey yelled. "What's wrong with me? What's wrong with me?" She stretched her arms to the ceiling and held them open wide.

Aubrey's phone rang, breaking her crying spell. She began to sob quietly, while rubbing her eyes to gain her vision enough to see who was calling. The caller ID displayed Scottie's number. Aubrey attempted to gain control of her breathing. After being unsuccessful, she decided to pick up the phone anyway.

"Hello," Aubrey answered in a shaky voice.

Scottie paused before responding, "Aubrey, is this you?"

She replied with little enthusiasm. "Yes, Scottie, it's me. You finally have time to call me, huh? Just to let you know I made it home that night. "

Scottie made another mental note about how familiar Aubrey was in such a short time.

"Oh, did I catch you at a bad time? I can always call you at another time."

Aubrey could hear the annoyance in his voice, but Scottie's cool nature would not let him explode on her. She took a deep breath and spoke a little sweeter. She had come too far to let her mother ruin her chance at a comfortable life.

"I'm good," she replied. "Just was wondering were you alright since I hadn't heard from you. What's up?"

Scottie noticed her correction in attitude and continued. "I'm calling you because I want to see you today. I have something I think is worth your while. Let's do dinner around seven o'clock tonight."

Aubrey listened to his proposition and was happy to be invited to dinner by Scottie. This time, she responded with more enthusiasm.

"I would love to accompany you to dinner."

Scottie provided her with the address and ended their conversation. Aubrey could not take the time to finish the lottor. Sho had bottor things to do. Her future awaited her, and she had to plan her new look for the evening.

* * * * *

Justin could not believe what had happened at Aubrey's place. He was coming undone, and he hated it. Justin was usually very composed and classy. He had never hit a woman before, and he was uneasy as to what may happen to him in the days to come. Justin could not believe Aubrey had strung him along and then dropped him for no good reason.

* * * * *

Trying to focus on work, Justin gave orders to his staff to place the flower arrangements just right and be sure the lounge area was ready for guests. A tall, slender girl in a uniform walked toward Justin as he continued to give orders.

"Excuse me. There's a gentleman at the front desk inquiring about Aubrey Green. He asked for the manager."

Justin almost lost his dinner. He feared Aubrey would call the law on him. That's why he called her numerous times to apologize, but now it was too late. Justin instructed his staff to keep working and then excused himself. Justin walked toward the front desk where the man in a blue suit and overcoat was standing. As he got close enough to see outside, he noticed an unmarked police car, which confirmed his fear.

With a lump in his throat, Justin greeted the man. "How may I help you, sir?"

Detective Torrey squinted his eyes as he read Justin's gold nametag on his lapel. "Justin Webber...hello, I'm here about Aubrey Green. My name is Detective Torrey. May I speak to you in private?"

Justin's face reflected concern; he just knew he was going to jail for assault. With white spit balls forming in his mouth, he mustered up the words to say, "Sure, Detective. Follow me."

The two men walked down the hall and made a right. Justin took him to the back of the lounge area where there was no one around.

Pointing to a cushioned chair, Justin said, "Please, Detective, have a seat."

Detective Torrey took a seat and placed a file on the table. Justin was sweating and becoming thirsty by the minute. Detective Torrey could tell Justin was hiding something, so he went with his hunch.

"Mr. Webber, when and where was the last time you saw Aubrey Green?"

Justin played with coins in his pocket as he reluctantly answered, "It was a few days ago at her place."

He paused as the detective just stared at him. Detective Torrey's stare caused Justin to fall apart.

"Look, I did not mean for it to happen. I am not like the animals you deal with, I swear." Justin broke out in a full cry, sobbing in between words. "I'm sorry. I just love her. I did not mean for us to fight. I just was trying to find out why she dropped me without warning. Oh no! Am I going to jail? Please, no. I can't lose my job."

Detective Torrey sat back and listened as Justin fell apart. He had struck gold. After shaking down Aubrey's granny he headed north to find her. He came to The Ritz Carlton because it was the last known address where Aubrey had received mail per his search. He played along with Justin to get more information.

"Well, I need more information and to hear both sides. I'm just the investigator, but if you want to be okay, I need you to take me to her home so I can mediate and gather both sides of the story. Cooperate and this can all go away."

Justin wiped his eyes and asked the detective to give him a little while to secure coverage in the hotel.

"I will be in the lobby. You have thirty minutes," Detective Torrey told him.

Justin stood up and led him back to the front lobby, where Detective Torrey had a seat in a comfortable lounge chair.

* * * * *

Aubrey pulled up to an empty lot. She looked at her text from Scottie to be sure she had the right address. Aubrey confirmed the address in her text with the one she had entered in the GPS system. The place was secluded and sat across from a lake. The light from the stars glimmered on the water. Across the lake, white snow adorned the roofs of houses. A concerned Aubrey called Scottie to be sure she had the right place, but he did not pick up. She decided to get out of the car and locate the entrance.

As she approached the building, she admired the architecture. The building reminded her of a well-put-together ancient Roman palace. The door was anchored by two gold columns covered in gold leaves. She grabbed the large handle on the door, and upon entering the building, she saw a white man dressed in a suit with white gloves on.

"I'm here for dinner reservations with Scotdale Boyd," she told him.

The white man extended his hand and replied, "Right this way, Ms. Green."

Aubrey was impressed that the help knew her name. She smiled and followed the gentleman through the lush space, catching a reflection of herself every few feet in the mirrors that covered the walls. The atmosphere was breathtaking. Plush velour seats sat against the walls, and oversized gold and crystal chandeliers hung from the ceiling. Aubrey was curious as to what the space was really used for, because clearly, it was not an open restaurant.

Straight ahead, Aubrey could see Scottie standing next to a table set for two and a long decorated table with fancy chafing pots and gold leaf ivory traveling down to the floor. She carefully took two steps down into the sunken dining area.

Scottie approached Aubrey to help her down the stairs. He admired her beauty as he helped her unwrap her shawl. Aubrey looked stunning in her formfitting evening dress. Her long, silky hair looked as if she had spent hours getting every curl in place. Scottie kissed her on the cheek.

"Hello, Bre. Welcome to our dining arena. You got all dressed up for me?"

Aubrey hated to be called Bre anymore, but she did not want to spoil the mood, especially after he shut down an entire establishment for their dinner.

"Well, hello to you, too, handsome."

They both shared a laugh as they sat down at the table. Scottie continued to make conversation.

"I'm so glad you were able to make it. I hope you find it to be worth your while."

After taking a sip of her wine, she responded, "I'm sure it will be. I'm glad you thought of me. I had fun the other night. I started to get worried that you had lost my number."

Scottie passed Aubrey the salt as he addressed her statements. "Oh no, I did not lose your number. How could I, when you're programmed in my phone?"

The pair laughed again.

"For real, though, I had fun with you, too. I'm just a busy man, always working."

Aubrey took a bite of her dinner roll. "I guess that's why they call you Scottie Blaze. You are on fire, blazing the trail for other black businessmen."

Scottie paused as he looked into Aubrey's pretty eyes. "I see you've done your homework. Not many people call me that. In fact, I thought that name was retired."

"I always research anyone who I spend time with."

Scottie moved his steak around on his plate as he looked up at Aubrey, who was feeling totally sure of herself. "Is that right? I usually do the same, but this time, your info kind of fell into my lap."

Aubrey's face transformed from a look of confidence to one of concern. "And what exactly does that mean, Mr. Scottie?"

Scottie proceeded after sipping his wine. "Why the concern, sweetie? It's nothing too bad. I had my suspicions even before I learned about your skills. I didn't peg you as an author anyway, no offense."

Despite his disclaimer, Aubrey was deeply offended, but wanted to know more. She knew if she snapped she would lose any chance of learning what Scottie was referring to. Aubrey placed her gold-tip silverware on her plate and then crossed her legs.

She threw her linen napkin at him playfully and replied, "Let me guess. I'm too pretty to have a brain, right?"

Scottie laughed. "I was speaking to my best friend Brooke and mentioned this new young lady that I met, only to find out she knows you, too."

Aubrey became defensive. She knew Brooke knew things about her that could mess up any chances with Scottie. "So what's that supposed to mean?"

Scottie replied, "Wait. Slow down. If I was offended by something Brooke told me, I would have never called you. If you're embarrassed about being a dancer in the ATL, don't be. I picked up on it the first night we were together. You moved methodically, to the point where you had my eyes only wanting to watch you."

Embarrassed, Aubrey did not know what to say. Her romantic dinner had turned uncomfortable. She could not escape her past no matter where she went.

Aubrey smiled and reluctantly responded, "Now why would I be embarrassed? I know I got moves."

Scottie came closer to Aubrey and said, "I'm glad you said that."

Aubrey cut him off; she had to get away. "Scottie, where's the ladies' room. I need to go badly."

Scottie pointed to the back of the building.

"I'll be right back. Hold that thought."

Aubrey stood to her feet and proceeded to the restroom. As she walked, there was so much running through her mind. She did not think Brooke had it in her to expose her because that meant exposing herself, as well. Or did she?

Aubrey forced herself to stay gone from the table for about fifteen minutes. She was not ready to have a discussion about her past, and she had a feeling Scottie was headed down that road. Aubrey had two goals in mind once she got back to the table: one was exposing Brooke, and the other was leaving on a positive note. Aubrey powdered her nose and headed back to Scottie.

When Brooke exited the restroom, she could see Scottie now sitting in one of the high-back velour chairs along the wall, and he had company. The chefs were breaking down the beautiful spread and cleaning the area. Aubrey approached Scottie and the two men who spoke English in a foreign accent. As she approached them, their eyes widened, and they both spoke in their native tongue while smiling at Scottie.

"Come on, Aubrey, join us. The chefs will be bringing desert shortly."

Aubrey was not in the loop as to what the gentlemen wanted and where they came from. Scottie pulled the seat close to him and patted it, gesturing for her to sit. Aubrey reluctantly followed his request.

"Scottie, what's going on?" she whispered in his ear.

Scottie patted her leg and replied, "Just relax, sweetie. I got you. Remember, I said this would be worth your while, and I meant that." He pointed his finger at the German chocolate cake that the chef had sat in the center of the table and then he addressed his other guests. "Come on. Please, share dessert with us. We are still waiting on two more people."

Just as Aubrey went to continue with a question, the light from the front door shined into the dimly lit space and they heard two voices. Everyone turned to look, and there stood Brooke and the doorman. Aubrey and Brooke's eyes met. Their scowl could start wars around the world. With her hand on her hip, Brooke transferred her attention to Scottie.

"What is this about, Scottie?"

Scottie was not interested in getting into their petty girl fight. He was all about business, and his next venture, World Tour Gentleman's Club, was going to be a hit. Scotty stood to his feet to address Brooke.

"Hello, Brooke. Come on in and have a seat! Let me introduce you to my two investors in my next venture."

Being as professional as she could, Brooke reached her hand out and greeted the men. "Nice to meet you," she told them.

Scottie continued as Brooke and Aubrey sat giving him the same look. Scottie looked at his watch, still awaiting one more person. He finally interrupted the silence.

"I see my associate is running late, so let me get started. I'm glad you all could make it. Brooke, as you know, you are my right hand in all that I do. That is why you're here. My next venture is a new spin on an old profession. My investors are here because they wanted to see a sample of the product that will be offered in the club."

Brooke cleared her throat. "With all due respect, Scottie, I understand that, but I didn't know you and Aubrey were that tight that she's accompanying you to meetings now."

Aubrey stood up, her blood boiling. "Why is it any of your business how tight Scottie and I are?"

Scottie jumped up and stood in between them. "Ladies, relax. If we're going to be working together, you two will need to get along."

Aubrey stepped away from Scottie and said, "Working together doing what?"

Scottie smiled at her. You, my dear, are going to be my featured act in my new club, World Tour Gentlemen's Club! You will be paid handsomely, and you will not have to do half of what you did in that old strip club you were in."

Aubrey snatched away from him. "Are you fucking serious? You called me out here to put me on the damn stroll? Who do you think you are? Paid handsomely? Please! I don't shake my ass for chump change. Did you see what I'm driving?" Aubrey grabbed her shawl and designer bag and headed for the door, while everyone at the table watched her storm off.

Before Aubrey could make her exit, Brooke stood up and yelled across the room, "Bitch, please! When did you get some morals?"

Aubrey turned and glared at Brooke, then Scottie. She shouted, "Scottie, maybe you should make your best friend the feature. She fills out a G-string nicely and can do things with her tongue that I never felt before!"

Brooke collapsed in her seat, and Scottie turned to look at her. Aubrey continued to the door, and as the doors were opening, she ran straight into Brenson. All of her belongings fell out of her hands. Brenson, who was staring at Aubrey's beauty, attempted to assist her. She bent down to gather her belongings and ran off. Brenson ran after her, but he was too late. She put her Aston Martin to the test as she increased her speed, throwing it into 3rd gear, while Brenson stood in the parking lot with his hands up and waving something. As the

201

car ate up the road, he appeared smaller and smaller in the rearview mirror. Scottie had just made a permanent spot on her shit list.

Aubrey almost banged out several times on her way home. She was furious that Scottie was like everyone else. He only saw her for her body and looks.

"I will show them all," she whispered to herself. "I will get published. I'm not just a pretty face. I'm worth more. I'll show them."

Aubrey pulled into her parking spot blasting Jay-Z's "Fade to Black" through her speakers. She put the car in park, got out, and stormed to the front door of her building.

Justin and Detective Torrey sat waiting for Aubrey to show up. Spotting her, Justin tapped Detective Torrey as he texted on his cell phone. Detective Torrey looked up and saw Aubrey walking away from her car as she hit the keypad for the alarm. His eyes widened when he saw the exact car that had almost hit him at the hospital in Atlanta, but Aubrey looked nothing like the woman who had been driving that day. Detective Torrey put his phone away, grabbed the file he had on Aubrey, and told Justin to follow him.

Aubrey was moving at the speed of lightning. She stormed through the lobby of her condo building and hopped on the elevator, not speaking to anyone. The elevator doors could not close fast enough. Aubrey made it to her condo and unlocked the door. Once inside, she threw her purse, shawl, and car keys to the floor. She yelled and growled to try to calm down.

She tried to think of the worst thing she could do to Scottie and Brooke. Scottie had to be dealt with no matter what; Brooke was just a bonus for her slick mouth. She paced the floor as thoughts of her entire day played over and over in her head.

"He wants to make a fool of me, huh? Calling me to dinner just to ask me to be his dancing hoe! I'll show him." Aubrey fussed some more as she headed to her room. She had some goodies left that could serve a purpose for torture.

As she headed to her room she passed her office and sitting room. Right pass her bed, she spotted the letter she had received from her mother. In a rage, she snatched it up from the bed and ran to the living room, where she turned the fireplace on and threw it in.

"Mother, screw you and your daughter Savahnge. If she comes near me, I'll show that bitch crazy!"

Aubrey turned on her stereo and connected her iPod. She scrolled through her playlists, and after finding the one she wanted to listen to, she let the speakers rip. She then continued to the closet where she had a bag full of weapons to plan her retaliation.

By the time Detective Torrey and Justin made it to Aubrey's condo, they hear loud music coming from inside. The men could feel the bass vibrating the front door. Detective Torrey knocked and then rang the bell. A scared Justin stood to the side out of visibility. Aubrey heard the knocks and doorbell, but decided to ignore it. She thought it was her neighbor asking her to turn down her music, and she was not in the mood for her complaining. She continued gathering her belongings and struggled with the big black bag. Aubrey took her shoes off to gain more leverage as she carried the bag.

Out of habit, Detective Torrey tried her door handle and found the door unlocked. He looked at Justin and said, "I'm going in. Come on."

Justin nervously shifted his weight from foot to foot. "I'll wait here until you talk to her first. She might still be too mad at me."

Detective Torrey opened the door and went in with his badge in his right hand and file in the other. As entered the condo, he saw a purse, keys, and a shawl lying near the entrance. The music became louder as he walked further in.

"Aubrey Green...Ms. Green." The detective's voice was drowned out by the music.

When Aubrey came from around the corner of the kitchen, she was startled by the presence of a man who was standing in her condo with his back to her. She dropped the black bag, and Detective Torrey turned to face her, his badge still out.

"Ms. Green, I'm Detective Torrey. I need to have a few words with you."

Her eyes fixated on his badge. She was sure they had found real evidence from Brea's murder. She traveled her eyes from his badge to his face, and that's when she realized where she had seen him, Atlanta Medical. He was the man that she almost ran over. Aubrey was sure he was out of his jurisdiction, and she became irate.

"How the hell did you get in my house, and what the hell do you want?"

Detective Torrey urged her to calm down. He noticed the bag on the floor that Aubrey had dropped, and when she bent over to pick it up, a black stun gun, wire, and handcuffs were visible. Immediately, Detective Torrey dropped the file and reached for his gun.

"Get up and put your hands in the air!"

Aubrey grabbed the stun gun with her right hand, and as she pressed the button while aiming, the wires shot out from the gun, hitting Detective Torrey and causing him to drop his gun. Detective Torrey knocked over a shelf on the wall as he fell to the floor foaming at the mouth. Aubrey quickly kicked the gun out of his reach. He twitched and gurgled as Aubrey turned the current up. Approaching him closer, she realized he wasn't moving any longer. She tried to drag him, but he was too heavy. As she stood up to wipe the sweat from her forehead, she heard a tap and a muffled sound at the door.

"Detective...Detective, are you ready for me?"

Aubrey walked over to the door so she could look through the peephole. On the other side of the door, Justin stood there looking like he had seen a ghost. This was her lucky day. Aubrey stepped back, grabbed a heavy statue from her mantel, and hid behind the door.

"Come in. We're ready!" she yelled over the music.

The front door opened slowly, and when Justin stepped in, he saw Detective Torrey lying on the floor three feet away. Aubrey swung the statue with all of her might. Justin fell face first and hit the floor.

Aubrey had to think fast. She was not sure how long Justin would be out. She closed the front door and proceeded to finish her job. She approached Justin and kicked him to be sure he was out cold. She ran to her black bag and retrieved some black rope. Then she ran back to Justin and tied his hands and feet together. For security, Aubrey placed handcuffs on his wrists, as well. Next, she searched Detective Torrey, removing his handcuffs and an extra clip from his belt holster. Aubrey prepared for when Justin woke up. She had a treat for him that she could not wait to give him.

* * * * *

Brenson was late for the festivities, but Scottie brought him up to speed. During the rest of the meeting, Brenson and Brooke barely spoke. Brenson was overly professional and only spoke about moving forward with the gentlemen's club. After about an hour the meeting was over and Brenson departed from his colleagues. Brenson held Aubrey's picture in his hand. He may have found the one other person in the world that hated Brooke and Scottie as much as he did. Brenson continued his trip, hoping he was met with gratitude instead of fury. Justin practiced his proposition that he would offer Aubrey.

* * * * *

Aubrey sat in front of Justin waiting for him to gain consciousness. She tapped her feet, growing impatient. Feeling that her waiting may take too long, she walked to the kitchen and fetched some cold water out of the refrigerator. She returned to the dining room, where she had Justin propped up against the wall. She walked in front of Justin and stood over him, enjoying how weak he was, when just a few days prior he had her off of her feet gasping for breath. Aubrey displayed a devilish grin as she threw the ice cold water in his face.

Splash! The water made a loud sound as it met his skin.

"Nap's over, punk-ass! Get up!" Aubrey yelled in Justin's face as he struggled to open his eyes.

He saw Aubrey standing in front of him and attempted to move, but was restricted by both hands and feet. He attempted to squirm out of his restrictive cuffs. Justin's eyes were totally in focus now, and he saw Aubrey holding metal wire and a clear plastic bag.

"What am I doing here? Aubrey, what the hell are you doing?"

Aubrey stepped closer and leaned down in his face, close enough to taste his breath. "I'm gonna need you to shut the hell up. Silence! You do not have the right to speak." Aubrey's country drawl got thicker the more upset she became. "Yo' bitch ass came in here a few days ago and attacked me. Now you want to ask me questions? Then you have the nerve to bring this punk-ass detective to my house!"

Aubrey walked over to Detective Torrey's body and kicked him. Justin turned his body so he could see what she was doing. There lay the detective motionless and not breathing. Justin began to scream like a little girl.

"Help! Help! Somebody help me, please!"

Aubrey bitch-slapped Justin. "Shut the hell up before I end this quickly."

However, Justin continued to yell. So, Aubrey walked over to the stereo and turned up the volume. The condo was well built, and the further back in the place, the less sound escaped. She returned to Justin and held the clear bag up in the air while laughing hysterically.

"You know this is ironic. You're going to die in the same place that you choked the breath out of me. I hope it was worth it."

Aubrey walked closer to him as he sat there crying with his hands behind his back. She bent him forward as he squirmed and fought to move his head away from her.

"I'm sorry, Aubrey," he sobbed. "I swear I'm sorry. I just didn't want to lose you!"

Aubrey laughed at his fear. She slipped the clear bag over his head, wrapped the metal wire around the bag at the base of his neck, and then pulled.

"I hope this pussy was worth dying for."

Justin turned red and then purple. His body flipped about wildly. In an attempt to save his life, he threw his body forward and knocked Aubrey to the floor. He fell on her from the knees down. Aubrey struggled to regain leverage. She squirmed from under Justin, never letting go of the wire around his neck. Breaking free and now angrier than before, she wrapped the wire around his neck two more times and did not let go until he stopped moving.

Aubrey collapsed on the floor while trying to catch her breath. As she scanned the room, she became overwhelmed with emotion. Hyperventilating and crying was her release. She slid backward on the floor, looking at what she had done. She was broken down and had no idea how she would get rid of two bodies that outweighed her three times.

As she slid back away from the two bodies, she came across the file that Detective Torrey had dropped. Shaking and with tear-stained eyes, Aubrey opened the envelope that lay inside of the file and began to investigate. She found a picture of herself, petition for a warrant, prison DNA results, a picture of what looked like her mother when she was young, and a newspaper article from 1984. The headline read: Wolves in Sheep's Clothing.

She read on: Store owner and school volunteer Rahieed Rohanm, 49, convicted for the rape of his stepdaughter Cynthia Green, will be sentenced in the Atlanta court in twenty-one days. Rohanm fathered a child with Cynthia, 17, eleven months ago. Since Cynthia Green has come forth, there have been five other teenage girls from his neighborhood that alleged inappropriate sexual conduct with Rohanm. He will stand trial for those crimes at a later date. In the meantime, Cynthia Green gave birth to a baby girl Aubrey Green, now two months old (shown in picture to the right)...

Aubrey stopped reading and began screaming to the top of her lungs. The picture of her rapist father stared back at her. It was like looking in the mirror, except for her grey eyes, which she got from her mother.

"I'm a product from a rape! I'm a fucking rape baby! Oh no! OOOOOOOO, my God! Why? That's why mama don't want me...she don't want me."

Overcome with emotion, Aubrey ran through her bedroom to the bathroom. She punched the mirror with her fist repeatedly, shattering the glass, and cried from the depths of her soul. Wanting to be loved had always been in her, but she could never reach that dangling carrot.

Aubrey picked up a jagged piece of glass and scrapped it across her right cheek, then her forehead. Blood sprayed everywhere as she cried louder.

"I have the face of a rapist!"

She dragged the now blood-stained shard of glass over her face again. As the loss of blood and pain took over, Aubrey collapsed to the cold bathroom floor and landed on a pile of broken glass. She could not keep her eyes open, so she gave up.

Chapter 16
Master Plan

Aubrey cracked one eye open and attempted to focus. Her head split from pain that radiated from the base of her neck to the top of her head. She attempted to open her other eye, but was unsuccessful. The patch that was snuggly taped over her right eye prevented it from opening. Aubrey used her open eye to attempt to make some sense of her surroundings.

She was in a hospital bed and propped up by pillows. She could feel an IV tube in her right arm and hear machines in the background. Aubrey attempted to yell out, but quickly realized her voice was too weak. She tried again.

"Hello...hello," she was able to whisper.

Aubrey leaned over the bed and tried to get a better look around. She was startled by a loud humming sound and the feeling of pressure on both legs. The surprise motivated her to get a few more octaves in her voice.

"Helllllo, where am I? Help me!"

The television volume went mute in the next room.

Aubrey yelled again. "Help me!"

An Asian woman came running in the room dressed in scrubs. Aubrey was in shock. All she remembered was falling on the bathroom floor bleeding after reading about her father.

The woman yelled, "She woke! She woke!"

The nurse ran around like a chicken with her head cut off, trying to find the telephone. She finally located it and dialed the number. Aubrey could hear her speaking in broken English from the other room, but could not make out what she was saying.

The nurse returned to Aubrey and began taking her vitals.

"Miss, where am I?" Aubrey asked.

The nurse patted her on the leg and replied, "You home. He will be here soon."

Aubrey gave her a suspicious look. "Who will be here? What are you talking about?"

The nurse did not answer. Instead, she continued to work on Aubrey. The nurse lifted up the bed sheets and tapped Aubrey's leg. Aubrey moved her left leg to the side, and the nurse removed her catheter. Aubrey yelled from the swift pinch. She then removed the leg massagers. Aubrey could hear footsteps approaching the room.

"Who is that, miss? Miss, who's here?" she asked, sure the cops were coming to lock her up for murder.

With a smile, the nurse replied, "He here."

Aubrey looked up with her exposed eye and could not believe what she was seeing. He looked familiar, but she didn't know him. She sat up as the nurse continued to work on her.

"Who are you? And what do you want from me?"

He reached out his hand and said, "Hello, I'm Brenson. We met a few weeks ago when you almost knocked me over leaving a meeting with my brother."

She became angry remembering what Scottie had done to her. "So, Scottie sent you here. Fuck him! He should have let me die."

Brenson approached her and attempted to rub her leg.

"Have you lost your mind? Don't touch me."

Brenson tried to keep his composure. He could not take her yelling and insults any longer. He held her arms and yelled directly in her face, "Listen! Calm your ass down. I could have left you for dead and left those two bodies in your living room to rot."

Aubrey was startled by his strength.

"I don't work for anyone, especially not Scottie," he continued. "I hate him just as much if not more than you." Brenson paced the floor as he told Aubrey the story. "I came here the day I saw you leaving from the business meeting. I had your driver's license and was just returning it. When I arrived, I could hear music blasting. I knocked and rang the bell, but got no answer. I saw your car in the lot, which told me that you were home."

Aubrey stopped him. "So you entered a person's house that you don't even know to return a license? This smells like bullshit to me!"

Brenson took a deep breath. "Okay, I was going to come in regardless. I really needed you to help me...and the door was not locked. So, I let myself in."

Aubrey began to have flashbacks and started to cry. "What did you do with the bodies? Who else knows? Where am I?"

Brenson attempted to console her. "Calm down. I took care of everything. I called some friends of mine that know what to do in those situations."

Aubrey felt like she was dreaming. She lay propped up in a hospital bed trying to make sense of what was being told to her.

"Brenson, Bren, or whatever your name is...I do not owe anyone, and I know that people just don't do shit for free. So, whatever you had in mind is not going to happen, and for the last time, where am I?"

Brenson walked a few feet toward the wall and removed the sheets. Aubrey's mouth fell open.

"You were in bad shape and had lost a lot of blood," Brenson explained. "I could not risk moving you, so I had your home turned into a hospital setting."

Aubrey felt like she was in the Twilight Zone as she looked around. She turned and said, "And here I thought you were a business square."

Brenson laughed and replied, "I'm much more than that. Just wait until you hear my plan for revenge."

Aubrey sat back and paid close attention.

* * * * *

Brooke was busier than ever. She buzzed around her office making sure she had all of the important details of the grand opening for World Tour Gentleman's Club order. She had already sent out press releases and scheduled the entertainment that would open the night. As she scanned through her electronic agenda, she was met with a smiley face in pink highlighter. She smiled and sighed. Brooke was definitely in love, and for the first time, she felt complete. The smiley face was a reminder to finalize her lover's getaway to Paris. She logged in to her vacation account and completed their reservations. Scottie had outdone himself and was more ambitious than ever.

Scottie was putting the full pressure on Brooke and Brenson to make the opening of his new club flawless. After all, that's what he was known for. That's why his name carried weight. People that frequented his clubs could expect luxury and a very different atmosphere. Scottie's name was what he coveted most. Being admired and respected gave him the feeling of love and affection that he lacked from his father.

It had been almost four weeks since the blow up with Brenson, and about three weeks since the spectacle that Aubrey caused. That night after Aubrey blew up and stormed out, Brooke was mortified Scottie had to find out about her past that way. After the meeting with the investors and Brenson, Scottie and Brooke had a long conversation, and she came clean about everything. She knew it was the right thing to do. She could not look in Scottie's face any longer and lie to him. She was prepared to lose him as a friend if her being honest resulted in such.

To her surprise, Scottie responded the opposite of what she had expected. He embraced Brooke, and they made love like their lives depended on it. The following morning, Scottie told Brooke that he wanted her for himself. He explained that he could have lost her forever if she and Brenson would have worked out, and he could not live knowing that she was someone else's. Ever since that night, they were inseparable.

Brooke broke out of her daydream and checked on all of the photos for the main stage. She had a hard task on her hands. She had to find twelve exotic females to be the faces of World Tour Gentleman's Club. Looking at so many beautiful women made Brooke remember that she needed to get her hair and nails done. So, she picked up the phone to call her stylist.

Before she could place the call, though, Brooke heard a tap at the door. She hung up and said, "Come in."

The door opened and Brenson walked in with a pile of papers in his hand. "Hey, Brooke, just wanted to go over the numbers with you and be sure we're on track for the grand opening."

Brooke smiled at Brenson and said, "Have a seat at the table."

Brenson walked over, sat down, and started flipping through the pages. Brooke still felt a little awkward around Brenson since their affair and huge fight. Brenson, on the other hand, acted as if nothing had happened after Brooke and Scottie became an item, which had Brooke a little suspicious.

* * * * *

Aubrey was up out of bed walking about. All of the machines and hospital bed had finally been removed, and the nurse was off of full duty, only coming about two times a week. Aubrey did not like that too much because the nurse's absence left her alone with her thoughts often. Brenson came over daily, and he continued to encourage her to move on.

Aubrey walked into the bathroom and decided she was ready to face her scars. She had been avoiding mirrors for about ten days since coming out of her coma. Aubrey approached the mirror and removed the black cover. Staring into the repaired mirror, she began to sob. Her once beautiful face that had held her prisoner was no more. She had a scar that traveled from her forehead, next to her eye, and straight down to her chin. It looked as if someone cut puzzle pieces into her face.

Aubrey wiped away her tears and walked out of the bathroom, returning to the living room where she curled up and continued to write. Her writing displayed a more edgy quality. She took her pain and poured it all into her latest work of art.

* * * * *

Brenson pulled up to the tall building and threw his keys to the valet. He opened his trunk and gathered his briefcase. Brenson was on his way to make the deal of his life. He knew his life depended on it.

As Brenson entered the elevator, he received a text confirming his deposit and transfers. Brenson watched as each floor number lit up. He reached his destination, and the doors on the elevator opened. Brenson checked in at the front desk and was whisked directly to the back in a modern corner office. He took a seat in a white leather chair across from an older white gentleman. The receptionist closed the office door and disappeared in the large suite.

* * * * *

Scottie rolled over smiling. He was happy that he finally was able to tell Brooke how he felt, and now she was all his. Scottie's phone rang, and he searched the room to locate it. He bent over and picked up his pants from the night before. There was his phone ringing away.

"Hello! Hello!" His phone broke up as he attempted to hear the caller.

Scottie loved his home out of the city, but hated the reception. He walked in the hallway and stood next to the banister. The static disappeared.

"Hello, bro!" Brenson yelled into the phone.

"Hey, Bren, what can I do for you?"

Scottie continued to deal with Brenson because he was his brother, but he definitely felt differently about Brenson knowing that he went after Brooke even though he knew how ho felt about her.

Brenson paused, trying to catch the tone. "Did I catch you at a bad time, bro?"

"No. What's up, Bren?"

Brenson continued. "I just wanted to run the final numbers by you for the grand opening. We're about a few days away, and you know I'm anal about this. Also, I have an idea of a way to save money. You're going to love it."

Trying to get back to bed, Scottie hurried him along. "That sounds good, saving money. I hope we're not saving quality, because nothing is worth that!"

Brenson chuckled. "I hear you loud and clear, bro. Of course not! I know how you feel about your name."

Scottie went on, "Well, that sounds cool to me. I will check you later on the numbers. You can email me the report, and I will get at you if I have any questions"

"Okay, bro. Will do."

Scottie hung up the phone and headed back to the room as Brooke was coming out of the bathroom. He grabbed her hand and ushered her back to bed.

* * * * *

Aubrey sat in her bed going over the plan that she and Brenson had devised. She still had not heard from the publishing house since Brenson met with them about a week ago. Since the publishing house would play a big role in her decision to go ahead with the plan, she started to get anxious.

Aubrey flicked through the channels to find something on television to watch. She was sick of staying in the house hiding from civilization. Aubrey became frustrated and threw the remote at the television. She heard the front door knob turning and in walked Brenson. He had gotten so comfortable with Aubrey's condo that it was like his second home.

"Hello, Aubrey!" Brenson said with a wide grin.

She crossed her arms and replied, "Whatever!"

Brenson stood in the middle of the floor with takeout bags in his hands. "That's how you treat a man bearing wine and food?"

"Screw you and that food. Where is my life? Do you have that in a bag? I want it back!"

Brenson walked to the dining room table and sat the bags down. "Guess what I have?"

He waved an envelope around in the air, but Aubrey was not impressed.

"What are you so happy about?

Brenson tossed her the envelope. "It came."

Aubrey looked down and saw the publishing company's logo. She smiled.

"Now you flash that smile," Brenson said.

Aubrey's smile quickly faded to sadness. "You haven't even opened this yet, Brenson. Why did you get me hyped? This can be a denial letter."

"Not this thick," Brenson replied. "They could send a denial on a sticky note," he added, laughing at his own joke.

"You better hope so, because your plan depends on it. No deal, no plan!"

Now sitting at the table, Brenson looked up and replied, "Are you kidding me? Have you read that story?"

Aubrey slowly opened the envelope, removed the letter, and began to read.

Dear Ms. Green,

I have read your manuscript "Reflections of the Ugly Truth" in its entirety. I extend an offer to publish your book exclusively in all countries. Please review the attached contract and have your agent and lawyer review it, as well. If you are interested, we need the last chapter of the book and the signed contract in our office within five business days...

Aubrey cried tears of joy. Her pain and suffering hadn't been all for nothing. However, her celebration was cut short when she looked at the date on the letter.

"Brenson, we only have two days to get this in, and that takes us to the day of the plan. You were supposed to be there." Aubrey was heated. She would now have to change her own plans.

Brenson paced the floor. "Don't worry. We can pull it off. I will set everything up and be sure to get your contract in on time."

Trusting his word, Aubrey went to her bedroom and made an important phone call.

She skipped dinner that night. She was on a mission that she only had two days to complete. Aubrey worked straight through the day and went over her contract several times. Her masterpiece was finally done, and she had a day to spare.

* * * * *

Brooke checked her list and triple checked the show lineup. She was nervous about the show going well. She did not want the grand opening to turn into just another booty bar. No detail was left undone. Even the waitresses were perfectly put together, looking like perfect pictures. Next, she made sure all of her and Scottie's things were packed and in the car for their trip. They were due to leave immediately after the party.

Brooke stared at Scottie as he slept like he had no worries in the world. She kissed his forehead and rolled over to get some rest for their big day.

* * * * *

It was finally Friday, and everything was in place. Aubrey had just come in the house. She removed the bandage from her face and tossed her keys in the dish on her table. She had been waiting for this day for weeks. She prepared her outfit and double checked the items that she needed to take with her. She had already met Brenson and placed her prized possession in his hands, her finished final chapter and signed contract. It was time for action.

Aubrey took her time with her hair and bathing; some habits die hard. She adorned her beautiful body with the outfit she had chosen for that night. Despite her ugly scars, she still was beautiful in the body. After putting on her black stilettos, Aubrey pranced in front of the mirror. She had not done that in such a long time. She knew what she was about to do and mourned her old life. In a weak moment, she picked up the phone and dialed her granny's number.

After several rings, her granny answered. "Oh my God, Bre, I thought you hated me! That detective came here looking for you and showed me some stuff that brought up such bad memories. I was just tryna protect you, like I couldn't do with your momma."

Aubrey sat and listened as two tears rolled down her cheek. Finally, she took a deep breath and said, "Granny, I forgive you. I'm finally free."

Then she wiped her eyes, tossed her phone into the toilet, and flushed. She grabbed her gear and headed out the door.

* * * * *

The time had come, and Brenson could not contain himself. He called the office of Star Publishing to be sure that CEO Edward Carr knew that he was on his way. He was about a block away from his destination, and he was so excited because that meant his plan was about to go down.

Brenson pulled up in front of the building and left his car double parked. He was eager to get it over with. He took the stairs to be sure he made it before it was too late. Brenson entered the suite and spoke to the receptionist, who led him to the back. He checked his watch and saw that the time was eight o'clock. He knew it was only fifteen minutes until show time. He smiled with satisfaction.

* * * * *

Brooke and Scottie arrived at the grand opening party together. The event was arranged for females and males. As they walked up the red carpet, the media stopped them to take pictures. Seeing Scottie in public with someone who he was romantically involved with was unheard of. The fact that it was Brooke made it more of a shocker.

Brooke sported a gold form-fitting dress that reminded Scottie that she was just as sexy as the World Tour Gentleman's Club girls. The pair arrived inside and was escorted by a half-dressed beauty from Brazil to a pair of red velour king and queen chairs in the front row.

About ten minutes after being seated, the party planner had the lights dimmed on cue, and the sexy all-female band took center stage. The crowd went wild as they stood to their feet cheering them on. They completed their last song, and the crowd chanted for an encore. So far, Scottie was thoroughly impressed. His crowd seemed to be having a great time and enjoying themselves.

The party planner addressed the crowd and thanked everyone for coming. She wished them a great and fun evening. While the party planner gave her speech, a tall, beautiful African woman joined her on the stage and handed her a note. The party planner read the instructions on the note and then proceeded.

"Ladies and gentlemen, I usually don't change programs, but I have been instructed to give a big welcome to our featured act to start the evening off right. This is dedicated to Scottie Boyd!"

The crowd roared and stood to their feet.

The music started on cue, and the spotlight hit center stage. The sounds of a snake trainer blared through the speakers as a silhouette of a shapely woman moved slowly across the stage. Men whistled as she bent over and moved snakelike.

Brooke leaned over and questioned Scottie. "What act is this, and why didn't I know about it?"

Scottie leaned in and said, "This must be the surprise that Brenson told me about. Chill out."

Brooke turned her eyes back on the dancer. She was nothing like the rest of the show. The woman swung her head in a circular motion; her long, black hair unraveled and her curls cascaded to the middle of her back. Dressed in an all-black lace wrap with a lace veil over her face, it made for a mysterious atmosphere. The men were on their feet and begging for more. Money rained down on the stage. No tips were expected that night due to the large amount of money people paid for tickets, but the men were feeling generous. She revealed her red lips, blowing kisses to the crowd as she continued to dance.

A ruckus at the door pulled Scottie's attention from the stage. The host approached Scottie and asked him to come to the door.

"What is this about?" Scottie asked. "Can't you handle it?"

The host whispered in his ear.

"What?" Scottie said, then stood to his feet and headed to the door.

The music became louder, and as the drum line came in, the seductive dancer faced her back to the crowd and made her booty jump to the beat. Brooke stood to her feet. She knew that butt jump was Aubrey's signature move. At that moment, the dancer let her wrap fall to the floor. The crowd went wild as her beautiful bronze skin was exposed. Completely nude, she turned to face the crowd. The men howled with desire.

"What the hell?" Brooke yelled.

Some female partygoers got up and started to leave. The dancer put both hands in the air, and the lights on the stage got brighter. When she pulled off her veil, screams rang out through the room. Aubrey's gruesome face scared all who laid eyes on it. Brooke stood frozen in time with her hands over her mouth.

"I'm fucking ruined!" Scottie yelled from the door.

Aubrey locked eyes with Detective Perez as she stared at her from the door. Then Aubrey bowed and yelled over the noise of the crowd, "Thank you for viewing the Ugly Truth!"

Aubrey disappeared in the dressing room and pressed the detonator as it counted from twenty backward.

* * * * *

Brenson rushed from the publishing office to try to make it to the car and head to his next location. He drove about two blocks before stopping at a traffic light. Brenson's phone rang twice. When he looked at the phone, he saw Aubrey's number on the screen. Brenson pressed enter and an electronic voice said, "Goodbye."

Brenson looked at the receiver as he heard a ticking sound. There was a pause and then BOOM! Brenson's car went up in flames.

* * * * *

The lights overhead went out, and the pilot gave his welcome. Aubrey could feel the plane leveling out as she removed her veil. She was headed to India to start her new life.

Slipping out the back door of the club before the big explosion was an adlib, but was worth it. When it all came down to it, Aubrey realized that whether ugly or beautiful, she would always choose herself over others. Being rich and published made for a bright future.

Other Great Titles from Johnson Publications:

Emotional Ties-*Jewelze*

Homicide City-*T. Real*

Blue Mirage-*STAR*

Bitter Sweet- *T. Real & Jewelze*

Inside Out-*Lati`a D. Johnson*

Inside Out the Aftermath- *Lati`a D. Johnson*

Inside Out 360- *Lati`a D. Johnson*

Scribes In Stilettos *Kia Rogers, Shakina Lewis, Lati`a D. Johnson*

Love Notes To My Father-*Diashon Johnson*

Slipping in Sin-*Sarah Jamison*

Echoes From Heaven-*Sarah Jamison*

Coming Soon...

Cocktales- *STAR, Jewelze, T. Real*

Savage- *Lati`a D. Johnson*

Get to Know Us...
www.JohnsonPublicationsBooks.com

www.ingramcontent.com/pod-product-compliance
Lightning Source LLC
Chambersburg PA
CBHW032042240626
47154CB00003B/1035